SHERLOCK &

A JAR
OF
Thursday

Liz Hedgecock

WHITE RHINO BOOKS

Copyright © Liz Hedgecock, 2016

All rights reserved. Apart from any use permitted under UK copyright law, no part of this publication may be reproduced, stored in a retrieval system, or transmitted, in any form or by any means, electronic, mechanical, photocopying, recording or otherwise, without the prior written permission of the copyright owner.

This is a work of fiction. Names, characters, businesses, places, events and incidents are either the products of the author's imagination or used in a fictitious manner. Any resemblance to actual persons, living or dead, or actual events is purely coincidental.

ISBN: 1539399230
ISBN-13: 978-1539399230

For Stephen,
because this one is entirely your fault

Chapter 1
A Job Interview

I checked the address on the letter once more and looked at the townhouse looming over me. Upper Wimpole Street was very grand. Perhaps too grand for the likes of me. I took a deep breath, straightened my tie, and reached for the ring in the lion's mouth.

The door opened noiselessly, as if it didn't want anyone to know. Behind it was a tall, thin man in a jacket and striped trousers. 'Mr Hargreaves, I presume?'

I bobbed my head, uncertain whether I should bow or not. 'That's right, sir.' The man's eyes rested on me till I wriggled. 'I'm here about the advertisement for an assistant?'

'Yes, yes.' The door's jaw opened wider. 'Do come in.'

The hall was beautifully furnished, but gave me no clues to the house's occupants. I took off my bowler hat and held it in both hands to keep from fidgeting.

The parlour was as anonymous as the hall. 'Please take a seat.' The man indicated a wing-back chair. 'Now, there are some formalities to complete. Your name is John Hargreaves, commonly called Jack?'

I swallowed. 'That is correct, sir.'

'You are an orphan?'

'I am.' What sort of job required an orphan to undertake it? Then again, I was not in a position to be choosy.

The man scanned my face until my skin pricked. 'You appear younger than your letter suggested.'

'I am of age,' I said, perhaps a little defensively. It was the truth, though.

'You have never been in prison, and are not known to the police?'

'No, sir.'

Sharp blue eyes bored into me. 'Most satisfactory,' said the man, after a pause. 'Now, are you fit and well? Can you run, and jump?'

'Er, yes.'

'Are you able to swim?'

I gulped. 'I cannot.'

'You will need to learn…' The man frowned and sat back while I wondered what he would ask me next. It was the strangest job interview I had ever had. 'And you can start straight away?'

'Yes.'

The man's face cleared. 'Excellent.

Congratulations.' He stuck out his hand and I shook it, thoroughly bewildered. 'Welcome to the household. My name is Mr Snell, by the way.'

I paused mid-shake. 'I . . . I thought you were Mr Molloy. The person advertising for an assistant.'

Something like a smile twitched at the corner of Mr Snell's mouth. 'Good heavens, no. I am merely a factotum. We will go and meet Mr Molloy now.' He rose and brushed his knees. 'Come, Mr Hargreaves.'

'But aren't you going to ask me about my previous work?' I blurted, thinking of the sheaf of testimonials in my coat pocket.

Mr Snell raised an eyebrow. 'It will not be necessary.'

We descended a flight of stairs at the back of the house. The crimson carpet was so thick that our steps were noiseless, but I couldn't see what lay at the bottom. Mr Snell must have sensed my footsteps faltering. 'I am aware that this is somewhat unorthodox,' he called back. 'Mr Molloy has his own way of doing things, to which you will grow accustomed.'

The bottom of the stairs revealed a long corridor. Wall-lamps cast infrequent pools of light, but I spied several doors leading off. The hairs on the back of my neck rose. 'I'm not sure I —'

Mr Snell put a finger to his lips. 'Bear with me.' He shuffled along the corridor and I followed him. What else could I do?

The door at the end revealed a small sitting room, like a housekeeper's room, crammed with furniture. 'Sit, please.' Mr Snell indicated an overstuffed sofa. 'Mr Molloy will arrive shortly.' He waved a hand at the easy-chair opposite. 'That is his chair.' He took a wing-back chair half-way between the two.

Why would Mr Molloy choose to meet us in the basement, instead of the parlour? My uneasiness grew deeper. But Mr Snell sat calm, hands clasped on the table. 'He'll be here in, ah, thirty seconds.'

I watched the hands of the ormolu clock on the mantel, and as the second hand reached the bottom I heard a sound like the opening of a huge stiff door. I cried out, and in that instant a man appeared in Mr Molloy's chair, a small, weaselly man holding two wires. On his lap was a box covered in dials.

'Afternoon,' he said. 'You must be the new chap. I'm Fingers Molloy.' He let the wires fall from his hands, and beamed. 'Pleased to meet yer.' He extended a hand, which was small and none too clean.

'Jack Hargreaves,' I said, getting up and shaking his hand automatically. My mind was in a whirl. 'What — what just —'

'Say hello to my time machine.' Fingers chuckled and patted the top of the box. 'Don't ask me to tell you how it works, I ain't got a clue.' He felt in his pockets, and drew out two slim black velvet boxes. 'Here, Snell, put these in the safe for us.'

'Of course, sir.' Mr Snell made to take the boxes,

but Fingers Molloy snatched them away so that his hand closed on thin air.

'Fancy a peek, Jack?' he said, grinning. He opened the lid of one box and snapped it shut, but not before I had caught a glimpse of a necklace set with diamonds and emeralds. Inside the second box was another necklace less ornate in style, but set with a pearl the size of a pullet's egg.

'Are those real?' I gasped.

'Oh yes.' Fingers put the boxes into Mr Snell's twitching hands. 'When you've locked these beauties away, Snell, take yourself for a turn in the park. I'll see you in an hour.'

'Very good, sir.' Mr Snell inclined his head and glided away.

'Come and sit by me, Jack Hargreaves.' Fingers Molloy indicated Snell's chair. 'I bet you've got a lot of questions for me, eh?'

'Well yes, Mr Molloy, I —'

'I'll answer your questions, if you answer one of mine first. Game?'

I put my hands on my lap. 'Game.'

'Right.' Fingers Molloy leaned close, and said, in a low voice, 'Why are you pretending to be a feller?'

My mouth dropped open.

'Oh yes, I knew pretty much from the moment I landed. Men don't yelp, nor put a hand to their chest. Watch that in future.' Fingers nodded. 'Otherwise, you weren't bad. You fooled old Snell, anyway.' He selected an apple from the fruit bowl at his elbow and took a huge bite. 'So you've still got the job.'

I decided I had nothing to lose. 'I ran away.'

'Go on.' Fingers watched me over his apple.

'I grew up in the workhouse, but as soon as I was old enough they sent me to be a maid. The servants bullied me because I was such a child, and I vowed to find a better life somehow. One of the lady's maids walked out with a clerk, and that gave me the idea. I practised my round-hand and sums, and talked to the clerk, though I got my ears boxed for it. I studied the newspaper for situations when I was meant to be blackleading the study grate. As soon as I had enough money saved, I got the train to London on my next half-day. I bought a second-hand boy's suit, supposedly for my brother, and cut my hair off. And I found a job as an office boy. The work was lighter, the money was better, and no one looked at me twice. Then, well, I kept going.'

Fingers whistled. 'You've done all right too, judging by your suit. Why've you left all that behind to come and work for me?'

I laughed. 'I answered your question. Now answer mine. What exactly is my job, and where did you get that jewellery?'

Chapter 2

The Restless Detective

I gritted my teeth as Holmes scraped a particularly grating discord on his violin, and avoided an exclamation with difficulty. While the noise is an integral part of Holmes's thought process, that makes it no easier to bear.

'Watson, I am sorry.' Holmes had lowered the violin and was regarding me with an expression akin to sympathy. 'I am disturbing you.'

'No, not at all. Please carry on.' I braced myself.

He chuckled. 'Watson, your endurance and your politeness know no bounds. I have assaulted your ears enough for one afternoon.' He laid the violin down.

'Another case will be along shortly,' I said, to try and cheer him up a bit. In truth, I was relieved his boredom found an outlet in cacophony, rather than cocaine.

Holmes closed the violin case with a snap. 'That is

not the problem!' He flung himself back onto the settee. 'I have more than enough to keep me occupied.'

'Then why the obvious malaise?' I retorted.

'Nothing is worth my time!' Holmes chewed at a fingernail. 'It is all hands in tills and cats up trees — well, not quite so bad, but nothing that a reasonably intelligent policeman could not handle. I am being distracted!'

'By Lestrade? Surely not!' I closed my paper. 'He values your time too much to abuse it. And he pays for it handsomely.'

'Precisely.' Holmes swung his legs down and I watched him pace with the regularity of a metronome. 'No, I should have said that *we* are being distracted. I have a distinct sense of things being moved into place — a nudge here, an adjustment there, ready for something unprecedented. And yet nothing is tangible.' He paused, and glanced at the calendar.

'I can guess who you are thinking of!' I exclaimed. 'Fingers Molloy!'

Holmes smiled wanly. 'Indeed. He is due to reappear a week today, if my calculations are correct, in the corridor outside the Jewel House, and we shall be waiting for him with a crowd of the Yard's finest.' He began to pace again. 'But ask yourself this, Watson; where has he been in the meantime?'

'Well —'

'There! You don't know, I don't know, Lestrade doesn't know. How can a man who commits a series of high-profile robberies just disappear?'

'Holmes, he has a time machine! He could be kicking his heels in 1832!'

'The machine has a five-year span,' snapped Holmes.

'Yes, but he could keep going backwards!'

Holmes smacked his forehead. 'Yes, Watson! Or, of course, forwards...' He gasped. 'What horrors await us in the future?'

'He's an opportunistic thief, nothing more.'

'Watson, how many petty criminals of your acquaintance have the use of a time machine?' Holmes paused, and cut in as soon as I opened my mouth. 'Exactly. Fingers Molloy is more than the cheery rogue he makes out to be. I thought he was a fool to let me catch him with the time machine, but now I wonder...'

'What, Holmes?'

'I wonder if it was a warning to stay clear. And I also wonder...'

I waited.

'I have had this feeling of the stage being set before, and not long ago. It was when we were engaged in the case of the Valley of Fear. I trust you have not forgotten it.'

I had not. The case was too recent, too painful to have faded. 'You mean —'

'Yes.' Holmes took a deep breath. 'I suspect that Fingers Molloy is in league with Professor Moriarty.'

***

'This is an unexpected pleasure, Mr Holmes,' the desk sergeant remarked mildly.

'Lestrade's in his office?' Without waiting for a response, Holmes strode down the corridor, and I followed in his wake. He rapped on the door, listened for a second, and entered.

Inspector Lestrade looked up from the papers scattered over his desk. 'Good afternoon.' His tone was polite, but less than welcoming.

'You got my wire, Lestrade?'

'I did.' Lestrade waved the flimsy paper like a flag of surrender. 'I have someone in the files at present. He won't find much, though.'

Holmes sat in the chair facing Lestrade. 'What do you mean?'

'Exactly that. Professor James Moriarty is an eminent professor of mathematics, and Fingers Molloy is a common criminal of little note.' Lestrade squared off the nearest pile of paper. 'I have arranged for a constable to escort you to the file room. If you don't mind, I have plenty to be getting on with.'

'Inspector Lestrade, do you recall an evening six months ago when I arrived at the Yard and entrusted you with an object?'

Lestrade grinned. 'St Edward's Crown? Of course! That sort of thing doesn't happen too often. You said you'd tell me how you came by it one day.'

'And the day has come.' Holmes gripped the desk. 'I took it from Fingers Molloy, who was in the act of stealing it from the Jewel House.'

'Oh yes, the business with the calling card. What was it again? "Fingers Molloy, Burglar at Large. No Job too Small."' Lestrade began to chuckle, then caught sight of Holmes's face and stopped. 'You have to admit, it was amusing.'

'He has a time machine.' Holmes's voice was low, and he forced the words out as if they caused him pain.

'A what?' Lestrade's eyes narrowed. 'Do you mean a travel clock?'

'No, I do not,' sighed Holmes. 'I mean that he can travel backwards and forwards in time. One minute he's there, the next —' Holmes snapped his fingers.

Lestrade laughed again. 'You can't expect me to believe that.'

'We saw him,' I said. 'He disappeared before our very eyes.'

'Nonsense.' Lestrade pushed his chair back. 'It must have been some sort of illusion. Burglars can't steal themselves away. I'll take you to the file room myself.'

The route to the file room lay through a maze of corridors and passageways. 'Here we are!' Lestrade sang, opening the door. 'Now, Huggins, do you have those files I requested?'

A pale, slim young man stepped forward. 'I do, sir.' He held out two buff-coloured folders.

The Inspector took them and glanced inside. 'As I thought. Now, Holmes, you may satisfy your curiosity.' He put the files into Holmes's hands. 'Give them back to Huggins when you've finished, won't you.' He left, whistling.

Holmes opened the first folder, labelled 'Albert "Fingers" Molloy', and extracted a few sheets of paper. 'Hm. Born in London 1840 to a watchmaker and laundrywoman, one of eleven children. Warnings for disorderly conduct as a youth, sentenced to three months in 1861 for acting as lookout in a failed burglary. Six months for pilfering in 1882. Arrested for house-breaking in 1885 but released on production of an alibi.' He paused. 'That's it.'

'And Moriarty?'

Holmes opened the second folder and held up a single sheet. 'Professor James Moriarty. Accused of various crimes by Sherlock Holmes, on minimal or no evidence. No police contact, saving that he gave a statement to police when his house was burgled in 1885.' His eyes glittered over the top of the paper at me. 'This case remains unsolved.'

Chapter 3

The Gentleman's Retreat

Fingers swallowed his mouthful of apple, and regarded me with his beady eyes. 'You want the truth, Jack?'

'Of course.'

He took another bite, and considered. 'All right. Those necklaces, I stole 'em. I'm a professional thief.'

I tried to keep a poker face under his gaze. 'And my job is..?'

'What did the advertisement say?'

I fished the scrap of newsprint from my pocket. '"Capable young man with office experience required as personal assistant to businessman. Duties light but variable. Salary generous. Apply in writing, PO Box 225." Don't you remember it?' I tried to pass the paper to Fingers but he waved it away.

'Snell wrote it. I leave the book-learning to him —

and to you, now.'

I studied the carpet while I formulated my question. 'And what else will I be doing?'

'You're the new Snell. He's getting a bit long in the tooth for these capers, so I've taken him off active duties.' Fingers lowered his voice. 'Don't let on I've told you, but I've rescued him a few times now on the job. Can't have 'im seeing out his days in Newgate.'

I gasped. 'You and Mr Snell went stealing together?' I found it hard to imagine formal Mr Snell as a thief.

'Ha! He taught me everything I know!' Fingers let out a throaty chuckle at my shocked face. 'Anyway, this chatter won't fill the pot. Get your things sent for, and I'll take you on a visit.'

***

'Where are we going?'

'My club.' Fingers put on a smart overcoat, silk scarf, and bowler hat. He resembled a weasel dressed for a party.

'Is it far?'

'Nah,' said Fingers. 'Down the back of Charing Cross Road.'

'And what's the name of the club?'

Fingers looked shifty for a moment, then grinned. 'S'pose I'd better tell yer. It's the Gentleman's Retreat.'

'I haven't heard of it.'

Fingers tapped the side of his nose. 'Only a select

few have.' He opened the front door.

Mr Snell emerged from the parlour, duster in hand. 'When should I expect you back, Mr Molloy?'

'When you see me,' Fingers winked round the edge of the door.

I had to hurry to keep up with Fingers' short quick steps. 'Who are we meeting?'

'A business associate.' He whistled for a cab, and said no more until we alighted at Charing Cross Road. 'This way.' He darted down an alley, almost knocking over a strolling accordion player. ''Ere we are.' He pointed to a small, shabby blue door.

'Is it safe?'

Fingers dug a sharp elbow into my ribs. 'Course! In yer go.'

My hand moved to where the door knocker should be, but there was none. No bell pull, no keyhole, no handle. I pushed the door, but it was firmly closed. 'How do I get in? Is there a special knock?'

'In a manner of speaking,' smirked Fingers. 'Here comes a comrade. Watch an' learn.'

A well-dressed man sauntered towards us. 'How do, Fingers,' he said, his eyes taking me in. 'New boy?'

'Yus.'

'Give a man room, then.' Fingers stood back as he pushed the door open and went in.

'I don't understand.'

'I've got a key too, and it's just like his.' He

paused, pushed the door open and let it fall to again.

I tried pushing the door exactly where Fingers had. Nothing. I tried pushing hard, I tried barely touching the door. Still nothing.

'See, Jack, in our line you've got to pay attention.' Fingers opened the door again, with no effort. 'What do you notice?'

'It isn't where you touch the door. That time your hand was higher.'

'Good. Well observed.' Fingers scratched his chin.

'It isn't how hard you push the door…'

'Yeeees…'

'It's . . . oh! The first time you did it, you waited to open the door! What were you waiting for?'

'Now you're getting somewhere!' Fingers rubbed his hands. 'What's the one thing that's changing?'

I surveyed the alley, and the accordion player came past. 'The accordion man! It's his tune, isn't it?'

'Full marks,' said Fingers. 'Now, I ain't teaching you the tune yet, 'cos I need to be sure of you first, but I'll let you in. Put your hand on the door.' I obeyed, and Fingers put his hand on mine. I listened hard, but was still taken by surprise when Fingers' hand pressed down, and the door opened as though it had never been locked.

***

'Mind the steps,' Fingers muttered as the door closed, plunging us into darkness. 'Banister's on your left.' I groped for the rail and edged my way down.

'Good afternoon, Fingers,' a disembodied voice intoned. 'Who do you have there?'

'Afternoon, Jameson,' said Fingers. 'I've brought a guest. I'll vouch for 'im.'

I blinked as lights flared, revealing a man wearing a dinner suit and a pair of goggles. He stood in front of a stout oak door.

Jameson pushed up his goggles and surveyed me. 'All right. Keep him close.' He stood aside to let us pass.

'Why's he wearing goggles?' I whispered.

'Night vision.' And Fingers opened the door.

My eyes widened as I took in the scene. Given the state of the front door, I had been expecting a down-at-heel tavern with sawdust on the floor. I had never seen anything like this.

The room was round, and everything was curved. Table-legs sprouted vines, and chair-backs and candelabras exploded in a riot of gilded leaves and flowers. The plentiful mirrors were set with bevelled glass, reflecting distorted versions of the club's few patrons. The walls were marbled in blue and green. It was like an undersea palace.

Fingers strutted in and snapped his fingers at a waiter. 'The usual, please.'

'And for your guest?'

Fingers raised his eyebrows at me. 'I'll have the same, thank you.' I hoped the usual wasn't too strong. My head was already swimming.

The waiter brought two pints of ale, much to my relief. Fingers checked his pocket-watch. 'He'll be with us shortly.' I took a cautious pull at my ale, which was excellent.

'Hey, there!' Coming towards us was a plump, cheerful man in a tweed suit, perhaps in his early thirties. I made to get up, but the man flapped a hand at me in mock-disapproval. 'We don't stand on ceremony at the Gentleman's Retreat.' He sank into one of the twisted chairs and raised his eyebrows at me.

'This is Jack Hargreaves, my new assistant.' Fingers explained.

The man held out a hand to me. As I leaned forward to shake it I looked into his bright brown eyes, and they pierced straight through my suit and short hair. Then they crinkled in a smile. 'Delighted to make your acquaintance,' he said. His hand was warm, and the pressure light. 'My name's Smith, and you'll see plenty of me. I'm a regular here.' He turned to Fingers. 'How's Snell? Not indisposed, I hope?'

'Oh, far from it.' Fingers took a long drink of his pint. 'He's minding the shop, 'appy as a pig in mud. Since business has been so good lately I've expanded my staff, and Jack is my new recruit.'

'Wonderful!' Mr Smith rubbed his hands. 'Now, do you have anything for me, Fingers?'

'Of course.' Fingers reached into his overcoat and produced the two velvet cases I had seen earlier. 'This was an easy one. Reminded me of the good old days.'

'Machine work all right?'

'Like a charm.'

Mr Smith snapped the cases open. 'Very pretty,' he said, stowing them in a long pocket. He slid a plain brown envelope across the table. 'Something to keep you going.'

Fingers ran a grimy finger under the flap, and extracted a wad of banknotes. 'Untraceable?'

'Of course.' Mr Smith watched Fingers pull a sheet of paper from the envelope and glance over it. 'All in order?'

'Oh yes.' Fingers rolled the paper into a spill and lit it at the candlestick.

'Need anything?'

Fingers considered as the flame advanced towards his fingertips. 'Not for this job. You might drop by and adjust the safe so's Jack can get into it.' He blew out the stub of paper.

'I'll see to it next week. I'm busy at the moment; the boss is keeping me on my toes. Speaking of which, on to the next matter. Time stands still for no man.' Mr Smith chuckled and shook hands with me again. 'Nice to meet you, Jack.' He strode to a table across the room and hailed the well-dressed man who had preceded us.

'So you steal things for Mr Smith?' I asked, as soon as we were alone.

'Not for him, for his boss.'

'But you steal to order, and he pays you.'

'Indeed I do. I was approached by Mr Smith two years ago. When he explained the terms, well, I'd have been a fool not to sign up. A house paid for, money in my pocket, and time to pursue my own, ahem, activities. Money for jam!' Fingers's satisfied smile faded when he noticed my expression. 'It's all insured, the stuff I'm asked to get. No-one's out of pocket except the red-tape merchants. Victimless crime, if you ask me.'

'And who is Mr Smith's boss?'

'They call him Robinson. I don't need to know more, so long as the money keeps coming, and neither do you. Now drink up, and we'll be off home.'

We travelled back to Upper Wimpole Street in silence. I could tell Fingers was vexed with me, and for my own part I was occupied in speculating about the mysterious Mr Robinson, and his purpose in keeping a retinue of thieves.

Chapter 4

A Bee In A Bonnet

Inspector Lestrade jumped as the two folders landed on his desk. 'What now, Holmes?' he groaned.

'There's a connection!' Holmes cried. 'Haven't you seen it?'

Lestrade pushed the folders aside and glanced at the detective looming over him. 'No, Holmes. Unlike you, I do not have time to theorise; I have crimes to solve. Solid crimes I can understand, not fantasies of vanishing thieves.'

'So you haven't bothered to follow up Fingers Molloy's arrest for housebreaking in 1885, and the burglary at Moriarty's house in the same year?'

'How many burglaries take place in London every year?'

'I wouldn't expect you to know, Lestrade, given the inadequacy of your records.' Holmes stabbed the buff folders with a long finger. 'This file doesn't even give the address Molloy's supposed to have robbed, or the date. How can you work with this lack of facts?'

Lestrade sighed. 'I'll get Huggins to dig deeper. Don't hold your breath though, we are very busy. And I'd wager money the two aren't connected.'

'I wouldn't,' muttered Holmes. 'Which reminds me, I need you to lend me some men for a few hours.'

'What?' Lestrade goggled at Holmes.

'No more than four or five, to be on the safe side.'

'And what do you need my policemen for, exactly?'

Holmes leaned in and whispered, 'Fingers Molloy is going to reappear at the Jewel House in a week's time, at five minutes to five, and I intend to catch him!'

'He's going to ride in on his time machine, I suppose.' Lestrade snorted.

'More or less. I'm not sure how accurate the thing is, so I am allowing for a margin of error.'

Lestrade shook his head. 'You've lost your mind, Holmes.'

'I saw it too!' I interjected.

'I apologise, Dr Watson, but you've clearly been spending too much time with Mr Holmes, and become infected with this foolish obsession. I am not going to waste police time on this.' Lestrade dropped the folders on the floor, out of sight. A small smile crept across his face. 'I see.'

'You do?' Holmes's face lit up.

'Yes. Both these men have slipped through your fingers. Now you're trying to connect them into some sort of criminal superpower, though we have nothing more solid to go on than a calling card.' Lestrade's voice was dangerously even. 'You're looking for the big one, aren't you, Holmes? The case that will cement your reputation, as if you weren't famous enough. I've seen it before, you know. Promising men chasing after glory, and finding madness. Take my advice, Holmes; stick to your bread and butter cases, and keep your feet on the ground. Good day to you.' Lestrade bent his head over his paperwork.

I had to hurry to keep up with Holmes as he strode down the Strand. My head was in turmoil. I believed in Holmes implicitly, but his giant leaps of reasoning had left me shaken. Could Lestrade be right? Was the time machine some sort of trick? Was Holmes seeing connections where none existed? I knew better than to raise any of this with Holmes, but a chill settled on my heart as my cheeks grew warm from the exercise.

On arrival at 221B Holmes cut off Mrs Hudson's expressions of welcome. 'I shall be in my room. Do not disturb me unless I ring.' He collected several cushions and the tobacco jar, and the bedroom door banged shut. I attempted to bury myself in the latest doings of Mr Pooter and his family, but every so often I found myself staring at Holmes's door. Dinner and supper came and went, with no sign of Holmes. I was debating whether he had fallen asleep when the door opened a crack and a wisp of smoke curled round the edge. Holmes walked into the sitting room and took up the paper, as more pipe smoke seeped into the room.

After five minutes I could bear it no longer. 'Well?' I said, lowering *Punch*.

'I shall write to Lestrade tomorrow and apologise,' Holmes said mildly, turning a page.

'Really?'

'Yes. I shall assure him that I have considered his words and concede that perhaps he has a point.'

I spluttered. 'Are you all right, Holmes?' I had never known Holmes to acknowledge Lestrade's reasoning. Frankly, this worried me more than his earlier behaviour.

'Never better.' Holmes turned another page. 'Tomorrow I shall busy myself with bread and butter cases, as Lestrade puts it, and achieve some results. Now, is there any supper left?' He rang the bell.

It dawned on me. 'You're up to something!'

'Who, me?' Holmes's expression could have rivalled a choirboy's for innocence.

'Yes, you. You're lulling Lestrade's suspicions.'

'Proving my worth as a solid detective. And I must do it quickly. We've only got a few days before we kidnap him.'

'What?!' My mouth dropped open.

'If Lestrade won't believe us, the evidence of his own eyes should do it.'

'I beg your pardon?'

'The time machine, Watson! We'll take Lestrade with us, and then he'll have to believe it!' Holmes's eyes glittered.

'What's the sentence for kidnapping, Holmes? What's the sentence for false imprisonment of a police officer?'

'Quiet, you'll worry Mrs Hudson. I hear her stealthy tread.' Holmes grinned. 'Trust me.'

I said no more. Holmes ate his supper with every appearance of carefree enjoyment, but his tension betrayed itself in his movements; the way his fork stabbed his food, the flourishes of his napkin. He was like a coiled spring.

Holmes cleared his plate and put his knife and fork together. 'Watson, I —'

'I don't want to know. I want no part of this.'

'You say it, but you'll come and help.'

'This isn't fair —'

'Sleep on it, Watson.' He rose, rang the bell, and retired to his room.

I went to bed shortly afterwards, and lay tossing and turning for some hours. Holmes was right. I could not desert him, however questionable his actions. I just hoped we wouldn't find ourselves in the dock.

Chapter 5
The Tools Of The Trade

Despite my misgivings, I settled into my new life. My bedroom was well-furnished and considerably less cramped than the lodging-houses I was used to, and once Mr Snell had explained the workings of the gleaming white bathroom, I luxuriated in a hot bath every day. Meals were cooked by Mr Snell, or sent in from a local restaurant. All in all, I considered that I had fallen on my feet.

I took care to be more guarded in my questions, and slowly Fingers Molloy unbent towards me again. In the basement room he taught me the accordion player's tune, and introduced me to the new tools of my trade; a glass-cutting diamond, a foldaway saw for padlocks, and a skeleton key which adjusted itself to fit any lock with a gentle whirr like a cat's purr. 'Ingenious, ain't it?' smirked Fingers. He unlocked the door, pushed the top of the key, and drew out a bare shaft.

'I've never seen anything like it.' I examined the key. 'Where did you get it?'

'Smith delivered the kit when I moved in.' Fingers slotted the key into his canvas roll, and wound the leather band round it. 'The time machine came later. And what a piece of work it is! Smith says they're working on a new improved version which can go back or forward a hundred years. Think of that!'

I could imagine landing in the middle of 1788 and a crowd of powdered wigs, but what could 1988 possibly be like, when marvels like this were emerging now? 'Fingers, what's it like to travel in time?'

'You sure you want to know?'

'Of course!'

'It's like going on one of those rides at the fair wot leaves yer guts behind.'

I groaned. 'Don't you find it even a bit thrilling?'

'I did, before I tried it. You'll see soon enough.'

'Really?'

'Oh yes. You'll be helping me in a small matter soon, and you'll need to work the beast. Wheel it over, would you.'

The time machine stood on a gleaming steel trolley, concealed by a fringed velvet cloth. I removed the cloth. 'So what do all the dials —'

'WATCH OUT!' yelled Fingers, and crumpled into laughter when I jumped back. 'Sorry Jack, couldn't resist.'

'Well, show me how to work it,' I said, rather huffily.

Fingers wiped his eyes with a large handkerchief. 'It's as easy as pie. See the big dial, marked Time?'

'I do.' The dial was set round with inscriptions, and two arrows, one pointing back, and one forward. The inscriptions went from five years to one, dwindled to six months, three months, one month, one week, down to five minutes, and then forward to five years again.

'Well, you set it, grab the two wires, and off you go.'

I could not believe it was so simple. Yet I had seen Fingers materialise with my own eyes.

'Come on, Jack, try it. It's half-past one now. Set the dial to ten minutes in the future.'

My palm was damp as I touched the dial and clicked it forward two notches.

'Don't worry, I'll come with yer.'

'But how can we both —'

'I grab you, you grab the wires.'

'Will that work?'

'Should do. Usually anything I'm touching comes back with me.'

'So you've never done this before?'

'Well, I've never had the chance. Old Snell won't have anything to do with the thankless contraption, as he calls it.' Fingers ran a hand along the top of the machine.

'All right. But we're coming straight back.'

'Oh yes. Now, I'll stand behind —'

I waited, but felt nothing. 'Are you still there?'

When I looked round, Fingers had stepped away. 'I hadn't thought of this,' he said, gruffly.

'Of what?'

'Well, I'm going to have to lay hands on you...'

'Oh,' I said. 'Well, where were you planning to grab me?'

'Is round the waist all right?'

'Er, I suppose so.'

Slowly Fingers Molloy's arms appeared and his hands clasped together in front of my waistband.

'You're barely touching me.'

'Well it's awkward, touching a, you know, a young —'

I grasped the wires.

***

I swallowed the excellent lunch which was in danger of reappearing. 'It wasn't so . . . so bad.' The ormolu clock said it was twenty minutes to two.

'The further you go, the worse it is,' muttered Fingers, snatching his hands away as if I were a hot stove.

'How far will we go when I'm helping you with this small matter?'

Fingers frowned. 'Three months, I reckon. That'll make yer guts do somersaults.'

I shuddered. 'Give me a couple of minutes, and we'll go back.' I dropped the wires, and sank into a chair. 'So what shall I be doing?'

'Well,' Fingers sat opposite. 'You visit the Crown Jewels, hang around inconspicuous-like, and hide yourself in the passageway outside by closing time. When I turn up, you pull a gun, rush any detectives or whatnot who may happen to be in the area, and make sure we both get away. Three months into the past should do it. We can hop to wherever and stroll out like tourists. Job done.'

The last part of Fingers' instructions washed over me. 'You're asking me to pull a gun on a detective? Are you mad?'

'If it's the only way to get past him and his monkey, then yes, I am asking you to pull a gun.' Fingers' voice was grim. 'If he catches me, I'm for it.'

'Who?'

'Sherlock Holmes.'

I gasped. 'Sherlock Holmes is after you?'

'He is. I managed to hoodwink him and nip into the future last time, but he'll be waiting at the far end, I know it.'

Now the world came into focus. Now I understood why we had taken a cab to and from the Gentleman's Retreat, why Fingers always sent Snell or me for a newspaper or a pouch of tobacco, why he spent most of his time in the basement, and scurried down there when the door-bell rang... 'So he's on your track?'

30

'Wouldn't be surprised. So long as I lie low, though, I'm safe enough.'

I cast my mind back to the story I had read in *Beeton's Annual*. 'But he lives in Baker Street, ten minutes away!'

'Can't be helped. I've asked to move premises, but Mr Smith's a busy man. Anyway,' Fingers stood up. 'We should get back.'

I pushed my chair back and went to adjust the dial. 'Ten minutes back?'

'Yup.' I clicked the dial.

Fingers cleared his throat. 'Jack, can I ask you something?'

I sighed. 'I suppose.'

'Why did you leave your job? Snell said you had glowing references.'

I was glad my back was towards him. 'One of the senior clerks . . . his daughter was keen on me. I decided it was prudent to move on.'

'Oh!' Fingers laughed. 'So you don't . . . like women?'

'Not in that way, no.' I tried to keep my voice level.

'And what about men?'

My laugh was more high-pitched than I could have wished. 'Dressed like this? I think not!'

After a pause, Fingers said 'Let's go back,' and put his hands on my shoulders. We arrived back in the same room at twenty-five minutes to two and Fingers dismissed me, saying that he fancied an afternoon nap. I repaired to the sitting room and picked up the newspaper, but I read little. I kept thinking of Fingers, afraid to venture out of his beautiful townhouse, and of myself, in my grey flannel and bowler, striding and hiding about town.

Chapter 6
A Close Shave

Holmes was as good as his word. During the next few days he solved the case of the Pimlico cabinet-maker, unmasked an embezzler, and retrieved the Pumpernickel rubies. I barely had time to note the salient facts before Holmes dashed on to the next case.

'You're not overdoing it, are you, Holmes?' I asked, as he erupted into the room, filled his pipe in a whirl, then collapsed on the settee.

'Not at all. Oh!' He rushed to the bureau, dashed off a note, and rang the bell. 'Billy, wire this to Lestrade.' When Billy had departed, Holmes rubbed his hands. 'I have told him we shall call at half-past three with some valuable information. Watson, is your Army revolver in good order?'

'Holmes, you don't mean —'

'Oh yes.' Holmes opened the drawer of the

occasional table and drew out a pistol. 'I won't shoot him, of course. This is merely for persuasion. He'll thank me for it later.' He cocked the gun and scored a bullseye on one of the curlicues which festooned the wallpaper. 'We may need to shoot someone, though.' Holmes sounded pleased with this notion.

I went to my room and inspected my own gun, hoping I would not have to use it. I watched the hands of the clock crawl round while Holmes smoked and twitched. At last he leapt up. 'Come, Watson, it is time.'

Our cab rattled the short distance to Scotland Yard, and Holmes instructed the driver to wait. 'We won't be long,' he grinned.

My heart sank with every step we took towards Lestrade's office. Holmes tapped on the door, and an irritable 'Come in!' followed.

Lestrade was in his shirtsleeves, his fingers stained with ink. 'It's all or nothing with you, Holmes,' he grumbled. 'I appreciate your help, but we can't keep this pace up.'

'Perhaps you should take a break, Lestrade. Get some fresh air, do a spot of sightseeing.'

Lestrade stared at him. 'Are you trying to be funny?'

'Oh, I'm deadly serious. I have a cab waiting.'

'Don't be ridiculous.' Lestrade's eyes bulged as Holmes drew his pistol.

'I did promise you valuable information, Lestrade.

Now come along.'

'You won't get away with this,' Lestrade muttered.

'Wait until you see what I have to show you. Watson, cover his back through your coat pocket.'

Lestrade walked along the corridor with us, stony-faced, and got into the cab. 'Tower of London, cabbie, as fast as you can!' cried Holmes, and jumped in after him.

The blood drained from Lestrade's face. 'What's going on?' He clutched at me. 'Watson, what is this madman doing? Is he going to lock me up?'

I disengaged myself from Lestrade's grip. 'Inspector, please try to remain calm. It is as Holmes says; he wants to show you something. I don't approve of the guns; but you wouldn't have accompanied us without them.'

'Too right I wouldn't,' retorted Lestrade, and lapsed into sulky silence till the cab stopped with a jerk.

'We have made excellent time,' Holmes observed. 'Inspector, we shall proceed to the Jewel House, and I would like you to use your authority to clear out any visitors.'

'Anything else while I'm at it, sir? A quick try-on of a crown or two, perhaps?'

'Sarcasm doesn't suit you, Lestrade.' Holmes patted his pocket. 'Now get moving.'

A few minutes and a hefty bribe later, the keeper shooed away a flock of clucking tourists. Holmes led the way in and the Crown Jewels sparkled away, just for us. 'Nice, isn't it? Like a private tour. But that's not what we've come for. Now the Tower is clear, we shall wait outside the room.' Holmes led the way into the corridor and paced around, frowning. 'He took off — here.' He marked a spot on the floor with his foot, and stationed himself nearby.

'Took off? What on earth do you mean?' Lestrade's eyes shifted between us.

'In his time machine,' Holmes said, patiently.

'Oh good Lord.' Lestrade put his head in his hands. 'You've kidnapped me at gunpoint to come and see a magic trick?'

Holmes shrugged. 'More or less. Would you like Watson to find you a chair? We might have to wait a while.'

'Yes, I would. If I'm joining you on this fool's errand I may as well be comfortable.' I fetched the attendant's chair from the inner room and Lestrade sat aggrievedly down.

We waited, and we waited. Half-past four came and went. A quarter to five. Lestrade fidgeted in his chair. 'Your magic man's a no-show, Holmes.'

'He could arrive at any minute.' Holmes spoke calmly, but I sensed the steel in his voice. 'Stay where you are, please.' He drew his gun, and motioned to me to do the same.

And we waited.

It happened all at once. With a sound like gears

grinding, Fingers Molloy, in a dress and handcuffs, materialised with his trolley almost on top of Holmes, who fell and grabbed Fingers' ankle. A young man thrust aside a curtain and ran towards them, waving a gun. Fingers put his hands up, and his eyes were wide with dread. But the young man shouted 'It's me — Jack!' and whistled a little tune. Fingers chuckled, and grabbed the wires of the time machine once more.

I shouted 'Hold it!' and pointed my own gun, but the young man took no heed. He was trying to prise Holmes's hands from Fingers Molloy's leg.

'Fingers Molloy, let go of those wires!' Holmes shouted.

'No fear!' Fingers cried.

I stepped into Fingers's line of sight. 'Fingers, drop them!'

'No!'

Lestrade stood up. 'Fingers Molloy, you are under arrest. Step away from that machine.'

'I'm not gonner!' Fingers wriggled in Holmes's grip. 'What are you arresting me for, anyway?'

'I'll think of something,' Lestrade said, grimly.

'Oh for heaven's sake.' Fingers dropped the wires. 'Happy now?' Quick as a flash he turned the dial back, cried 'Grab on, Jack!' and seized the wires.

The three of them vanished.

Lestrade and I gawped at the empty floor. 'He's — he's gone!' quavered Lestrade.

The vast creaking sound came again, and the trio reappeared, looking seasick. The young man Jack let go of Holmes and pointed the gun at his head. 'Step back.'

A slow smile spread across Holmes's face. 'You wouldn't dare.'

The young man moved the gun left a little, and fired. Holmes reeled backwards, clapping a hand to his ear.

'Blimey, Jack!' said Fingers Molloy. 'Hold on, now.' And they disappeared.

I ran to Holmes. 'Let me see.' I led him to the chair. Blood poured from his earlobe. 'It's not too bad. Only a nick.'

'As I suspected,' said Holmes, wincing as I applied pressure with a handkerchief. 'Well, Lestrade, was that worth seeing?'

'I should say so,' breathed Lestrade. 'Where have they gone?'

'Far enough back to escape, I imagine.'

Lestrade walked towards Holmes and stuck out a hand. 'I apologise for doubting you, Holmes. If I hadn't seen it with my own eyes…'

Holmes shook Lestrade's hand. 'No hard feelings?'

'Not at all. If you're up to it, Holmes, I propose we return to the Yard. I want a full statement of everything you know about Fingers Molloy. The sooner he and his dangerous young accomplice are behind bars, the better.'

Chapter 7

The Pricking Of My Thumbs

My stomach lurched again as we plunged into the past. I closed my eyes and opened them to darkness. I shivered, and the gun in my hand fell to the floor with a clatter.

'Careful, now,' warned Fingers. 'Don't go shooting yourself in the foot.' He chuckled. 'You're a cool customer and no mistake, winging Sherlock Holmes like that. Now, can you get at my tool-roll? It's in my right-hand trouser pocket.' I groped my way towards Fingers and busied myself among his skirts. 'Good.' A tiny beam of torchlight revealed the same passageway, the same draperies we had stood among moments ago. Fingers put the torch on the floor, selected a lock-pick from his roll, and began to work on the handcuffs.

I retrieved the gun and replaced it in its holster, hoping Fingers wouldn't notice how much my hand trembled. I had shot Sherlock Holmes! Next time Fingers asked me to take a gun — I pushed my hair back from my clammy forehead. There would not be a next time.

The handcuffs clanked to the floor. 'Let's go.' Fingers pulled the dress over his head and wrapped it around the time machine.

'Why are you wearing that?' I asked, glad of the distraction.

Fingers pushed the trolley into an alcove. 'I had orders to steal St Edward's Crown. Seemed best to sneak in as a cleaning lady.'

'Oh.' I rolled this round my brain as we groped our way along. 'But how could Mr Smith — or Mr Robinson — dispose of a crown?'

'Maybe they were planning to melt it down,' Fingers mused. 'Never thought of it like that. I just follow orders and pocket the proceeds. Here, hold this.' He passed me the wrapped machine and pulled out his skeleton key.

We emerged into a London fog. 'Jolly good,' said Fingers, and whistled for a cab.

'But what month is it? What day is it?'

'Doesn't matter. We'll get a cab home and Snell will fill us in. I'll have to vouch for you, though. I suspect he won't have met you yet. In fact, that's probably why he gave you the job. Remembered you, you see.'

We arrived home without further incident, and

shortly afterwards, slightly nauseous, we arrived back in the present. 'Well, I'm done in,' yawned Fingers, although it was still light outside. 'Time for bed.'

'Fingers...' He paused, mid-stretch. 'Is it always like that?'

'What, nearly getting caught? No fear!' Fingers scoffed. 'That's the closest I've come, by a long shot. Anyway I'm dealing in different goods now, mostly.'

'No more crowns, then.'

'Couldn't risk it, they'd spot me a mile off. No, nowadays I specialise in metals more precious than gold.'

I racked my brains. 'Platinum?'

'Nothing so ordinary. The kind of metals you find in a laboratory. Needs a sharp eye to find 'em and a steady hand to get 'em. And what's a few ounces between friends?' Fingers laughed at my puzzled expression. 'Sleep on it, Jack. And well done. Got me out of a tight spot, you did.' He patted me on the shoulder.

I lay awake for some time. I could sense the gun's presence, in the bottom drawer of the bureau, muffled in a shirt. I remembered Sherlock Holmes's hands round Fingers' ankle like an eagle's claws, hands which did not let go however much I pulled and pinched. *You panicked*, I told myself. *You panicked, and that was why you fired at him. It could have been much worse.*

I didn't want it to get *any* worse. And now Mr

Holmes and the other two men — Dr Watson? One of the Inspectors? — had seen me, I would have to lie low, like Fingers. My days of strolling in the park and window-shopping were done. Or I could go to the train station tomorrow, and travel out of their reach...

On the run again, Jack, said the little voice in my head. I batted it away. That was what any sensible person would do. I turned my pillow and myself over.

Yet I still could not sleep. What might those metals be? I rose, changed into a loose shirt and trousers, and went to the sitting room. Apart from the sound of Snell pottering in the kitchen below, the house was silent. I drew an encyclopaedia from the bookshelf, and settled to read.

Metals. Metallurgy. Metalworking.

It was hopeless. While I had taken care to study the sorts of things a smart young clerk should know, my grasp of anything but the most popular science was shaky. I replaced the encyclopaedia and a battered cookery book caught my eye. Mrs Beeton. *Beeton's Christmas Annual. A Study in Scarlet.* Did *everything* have to lead to Sherlock Holmes? I went back to bed in disgust.

After some hours of sleep, the world appeared brighter the next morning. When I arrived in the dining room Fingers was already tucking into a hearty plate of ham and eggs. 'Morning, Jack,' he said, chewing. 'You'd best buck up. Smith's wired to say he'll be round at nine-thirty to see to the safe.' He tapped the telegram in front of him, which I noticed was addressed to Mr Snell. Another example of Fingers lying low, I presumed.

'I'll place an order with Mr Snell,' I said, and hurried to the kitchen. My stomach was turning somersaults, and I hoped it was due to hunger.

Fifteen minutes and a mostly-uneaten plate of food later, I inspected myself in the bedroom glass. An impulse had made me change into my Sunday shirt. My hair brushed the collar at the back. *I must get it trimmed.* The jangle of the door-bell made me snap to attention. I smoothed my hair back and hurried downstairs.

Mr Smith was hanging his coat on the stand, and Mr Snell hovered nearby. 'Ah, Jack, isn't it?' He extended his hand and again, the gentle, warm, enclosing clasp. 'I knew I would be passing, so here I am!'

Fingers emerged from the basement. 'Hello, Mr Smith.'

'Good morning, Fingers. Now, where does your safe live?'

'Down 'ere.' We followed Fingers into the corridor. Half-way along he stopped so abruptly that we nearly fell over him, and touched a knot in the wooden panelling. The panel slid back, revealing a squat black safe.

'Ah, yes,' said Mr Smith, and knelt before it.

'Where's the lock?' I asked. There was neither

keyhole nor dial, only a round disc of bright metal in the middle of the door.

Mr Smith placed his thumb on the disc, and the door swung open.

'Clever, ain't it?' smirked Fingers.

'Clever it may be,' said Mr Smith, 'but you and Snell are standing in my light. Would you be so kind as to give me some room? In fact, a cup of tea would help the job on tremendously.'

We watched their retreating backs. 'Now, Jack, I want your thumbprints.' Mr Smith drew a small notebook from his pocket; when he opened it the leaves were not paper, but celluloid. 'Place a thumb on each page, please.'

I stuck my thumbs out and reached forward, and the time machine and the shooting and the nausea and Holmes's grip charged through my head. 'What! You're shaking.' Mr Smith snapped the book shut. 'Are you nervous?'

'It's nothing,' I said, my cheeks burning.

'Is it?' My shoulder burned too, where his hand touched it. 'Jack, you could find a more suitable situation, I am sure.'

'Mr Molloy has been very kind,' I stammered.

'I daresay he has. However, there is another opening. A less — action-oriented role, reporting directly to me.'

'I'm not sure I understand, sir,' I gulped.

'Oh, you could pick it up.' Mr Smith's hand

brushed my neck and he twirled a strand of my hair around his fingers. I felt as though flames were licking all over me. 'Perhaps you will think about it for me.'

I was losing the ability to think at all. 'Please —' I reached to dislodge his fingers, and my hand was in his clasp before I knew it.

'I shall let you consider it, for now.' His bright brown eyes looked into mine. 'I have a feeling you — and I — would enjoy it. Don't mention it to Fingers, but do keep it in mind . . . Jack.' I felt as if a furnace door had opened an inch away.

He drew back as Mr Snell appeared, wearing an apron and carrying a tea-tray. 'Ah, Snell. Most kind of you, but I fear I must be getting on. I have brought the wrong equipment, so I shall have to call round again. Give my regards to Fingers. Jack, I shall see you again soon.' Mr Smith met my eye for a second, nodded, and walked off, whistling.

'Well!' Mr Snell exclaimed when the front door had closed. 'That's most unlike Mr Smith. He never forgets anything. A model of efficiency, that's him.'

I put my palms on the cool dark wood panelling. 'What does he do exactly, Snell?'

'He's a middleman, I believe. He answers to Mr Robinson, and that's as much as I know. Are you going after his job, Jack?'

I shook my head violently, and Mr Snell laughed. 'Well, I'll drink his tea if he doesn't want it. Fancy a cup?'

I nodded, afraid to trust my voice, and we walked back to the kitchen together. I stayed near the fire to account for my burning cheeks, and wondered why Mr Smith liked me, and what I ought to do. My heart thumped in my chest, my head ached, and my conscience prickled me.

Chapter 8
A Case Of Identity

Despite our best efforts, Holmes and I could furnish Lestrade with merely a few pages of material. Lestrade had already heard most of it, dismissing it as the ravings of an obsessive, but this time he wrote it all down. 'I wish we had more to go on,' he said regretfully, tapping the page with his fountain pen. 'When we investigated the Aston and Coutts Bank robberies both places were clean as a whistle, apart from Molloy's calling card.' He chewed the end of his pen. 'I can get Huggins to dig into the files for those minor offences. It might give us some intelligence on his associates.'

'It might,' said Holmes. 'It won't help.'

'Why not?' Lestrade snapped his notebook shut. 'It's all we can do.'

'Yes,' said Holmes. 'But that doesn't make it worth doing.'

'Well, what do you propose instead?'

'Thinking.' Holmes said. 'The other crimes on Fingers Molloy's file are common-or-garden matters. Mansions, banks and the Crown Jewels are entirely different beasts. Either Fingers Molloy has had a sudden attack of extreme ambition, or…'

'What? What?' Lestrade leaned forward, as did I.

'Or another man is behind these robberies, and Molloy is merely his agent.' Holmes said no more, but the word *Moriarty* stood out as though it were stamped on his forehead.

'What about that young man, now?' Lestrade frowned. 'Did either of you get a good look at him?'

'Hardly,' said Holmes. 'It was dark, and he was bent over my hands, except when he was pointing a gun at my head. I am afraid I was less than interested in his appearance at that moment.'

I shook my head. 'I wouldn't know him again.'

'Wonderful,' sighed Lestrade. 'An unremarkable young man named Jack. No shortage of those in London.'

'A young man with a common name, who strives to be unremarkable, enjoys popular literature, and has been employed as a clerk for some years before throwing his lot in with Fingers Molloy quite recently,' mused Holmes.

'How on earth…?' Lestrade and I goggled at Holmes.

'When Jack ran on to the scene, he had to tell

Fingers who he was. That implies that he was not known to Fingers six months ago, at the start of the time machine's journey. Furthermore, when Jack was trying to loosen my grip I noticed a pronounced writer's callus on the middle finger of his right hand. He cannot have been away from his occupation long. I deduce his interest in popular fiction as he recognised me immediately.'

'Oh!' Lestrade uncapped his pen. 'And the unremarkability?'

'Well, none of us can describe him. All I myself can contribute was that he has dark hair, cut in a common style, and regular features. His clothes were, well, exactly what I would expect a smart young clerk to be wearing. Although there is one thing...'

'Yes?' Lestrade prompted, pen poised.

'His suit was of good quality; I felt the material brush against my hands. It was also in the current fashion; I made out the small lapels. But its fit was not quite right. The shoulders were too broad. A smart young man like Jack would get a tailor or a seamstress to alter it.'

'He might have bought it secondhand, or not have had time —' I reasoned.

Holmes laughed. 'Perhaps I am grasping at straws in my attempt to winkle Jack out of his haystack.' He stretched, then stood. 'I shall ponder the matter further at Baker Street, as we have all worked hard enough for one day.'

'True,' yawned Lestrade. 'Tomorrow is time enough to set Huggins on the files.'

Back at 221B, Holmes allowed Mrs Hudson to fuss over him and to bring us a fine cold collation for supper. 'Straight to bed when you're finished,' she said. 'Dr Watson, I trust you to make Mr Holmes behave himself.'

'I shall.' Truthfully, I was more than ready for my bed.

The next morning I was surprised to find myself out of bed before Holmes, who was usually an early riser when on a case. I would like to say that I enjoyed an excellent breakfast, but it was marred by my constant glances at Holmes's bedroom door. He emerged clad in a dressing gown just after half-past nine.

'Are you all right, Holmes?' I enquired.

Holmes took a piece of toast from the rack. 'Absolutely, and ready for breakfast.' He buttered his slice lavishly, and devoured it. 'I could not do justice to supper last night after the severe case of *mal de mer* induced by that infernal machine.' He rang the bell.

'What was it like, travelling through time?'

Holmes considered, reaching for more toast as he did so. 'It was like falling a great distance and being brought up short an inch from the ground. Going the other way was the same, in reverse.'

I shuddered.

'Quite. It isn't something I should care to do again, though I am usually an excellent traveller.'

'They didn't enjoy it, either,' I commented. 'You all appeared as ill as each other.'

'Interesting.' Holmes motioned to me to pass the butter. 'That suggests they don't use the machine often enough to get accustomed to it. Perhaps we have some breathing space while they plan their next excursion.'

Mrs Hudson arrived and Holmes ordered a huge breakfast. 'I feel an unfamiliar need for brain food,' he said, leaning back in his chair and putting his hands behind his head. 'That, and tobacco.'

'You are not placing your faith in Lestrade's files, then.'

Holmes snorted. 'Lestrade will seek connections which are logical and sensible. This is not that sort of case.'

After breakfast I went to my practice, which I had sadly neglected for the past few days, and dealt with a host of mundane ailments. How refreshing to be back in the real world, I thought, as I drove to make the day's house calls. I was occupied until past four o'clock, and I repaired to Baker Street with a pleasant sense that I had fulfilled my duty.

As the cab drew up outside 221B the door opened, and a figure was silhouetted in the gaslight. A late caller for Holmes, no doubt. I paid the cabman, and when I turned back to the house the figure was still on the step, talking with Billy and gesturing; a man of medium height, wearing an ulster. I resolved to offer assistance.

'Excuse me.' The man turned at my voice. Surely —

He let out a horrified gasp and tried to push past me, but I seized his arm and twisted it till he screamed. 'Trying for another shot, are you?'

'He won't give his name, sir!' cried Billy. 'He keeps saying he has to see Mr Holmes alone —'

'Check his pockets, Billy.' Billy advanced, but the miserable fellow was wriggling too much for him to get close. 'Never mind. We'll bring him in. Run and tell Mr Holmes we have an unexpected visitor, named Jack.'

Chapter 9

The Lion's Den

'What about your Hippocratic oath, Dr Watson?' I shouted as he marched me into the hallway. '"First do no harm", remember?'

'You should have considered that before you took a pot-shot at my friend.' Dr Watson's voice was low and full of venom, and I winced as he bent my arm round a little more.

A door overhead banged, and footsteps came closer. I struggled, but Dr Watson's grip never shifted.

Sherlock Holmes appeared on the landing and stared at me. He had a small piece of gauze on his ear.

'Would you mind lending a hand, Holmes, if you have a moment?' Dr Watson's teeth were clenched. 'We have a slippery customer.'

Mr Holmes charged down the stairs. 'Will you come quietly, or do I have to use force?' I shrank back from his fury.

'I'll come quietly! I will!' I cried.

'You had better. Stand still, if you please.' I complied, and Dr Watson's grip slackened a fraction.

'Are you armed?' I shook my head violently.

Sherlock Holmes's eyes gleamed. 'I shall check, to be on the safe side.' He reached into my left coat pocket, then my right. 'Clear so far,' he commented, and his hands moved towards my buttons.

'No!' I yelped. 'Let me take it off!'

He laughed. 'I think not.' He touched the front of my coat — and I couldn't help it. I screamed.

Sherlock Holmes snatched his hands away. 'Watson, loosen your grip.'

'Holmes, he's dangerous and probably armed!'

'Loosen it, I say!' snapped Mr Holmes.

'What is going on?' A woman followed the exclamation up the kitchen stairs, holding a potato in one hand and a knife in the other. She stopped dead, staring at me in complete confusion. 'I thought I —'

'You did, Mrs Hudson,' said Sherlock Holmes. 'You heard a woman scream.'

'Good Lord,' exclaimed Dr Watson, and his grip slackened. I should have torn myself away and made a dash for the front door, but my legs gave way and I would have sunk to the floor if he had not kept hold of me.

'Jack,' Mr Holmes said, not unkindly, 'will you permit Mrs Hudson to check your pockets for weapons?'

I nodded. There seemed no point in refusing.

Mrs Hudson handed the potato and knife to Billy, then unbuttoned my coat, patted my trouser and waistcoat pockets, and checked my boots. 'I can't find anything, Mr Holmes.' She stepped back.

'Good.' I could sense Sherlock Holmes's eyes on me, though all I could see was a watery version of the hall carpet. 'I suggest we go to my consulting-room. Mrs Hudson, please arrange some tea.' He strode off without waiting for an answer.

'Can you stand?' said Dr Watson.

'Yes,' I gulped.

'I shall keep a hand on your collar. I would rather not, but given the circumstances...' His fingers slid between my collar and my neck, and we mounted the stairs.

Sherlock Holmes stood on the landing, holding a pistol. 'On the settee please, Watson.' Dr Watson steered me to the chesterfield. I sank onto it and tears poured out of me till I thought I might dissolve.

'Crying won't help you,' scolded Dr Watson.

'Let her be for a minute or two.' My sobs rang in the silent room, and the sound was enough to make me check them in shame. Eventually I managed to take deeper breaths between each sob, wipe my eyes and, at last, quieten myself.

'So, what are you doing here, alone and unarmed?' Mr Holmes was studying me as he might a museum exhibit. 'I must say I am somewhat surprised by your call. I did not expect to encounter you again for a while.' He smiled. 'I suppose I ought to thank you for not killing me, although I was less than grateful at the time.'

'For heaven's sake, Holmes, she shot you!' Dr Watson exclaimed. 'I'm going to call a policeman and get her taken to the cells. Let Lestrade deal with her.' He went to the window.

'No!' Sherlock Holmes and I shouted in unison. Dr Watson paused, his hands on the sash.

'Watson, don't you see?' Mr Holmes continued, more quietly. 'She could have killed me, but did not. She is a new recruit to Fingers Molloy's team. And she has turned up on our doorstep unarmed. That can only mean one thing.'

'What?' demanded Watson, his hands still on the sash.

'She has come to us with information.'

'Or she is hoping to feed you a pack of lies,' sneered Dr Watson.

'I'm not, I swear it!' In my agitation I rose to my feet, but Mr Holmes motioned at me with his pistol to sit.

A gentle tap sounded at the door and Mrs Hudson entered with a tea-tray. 'I trust everything is under control,' she remarked, eyeing Mr Holmes's gun. She put the tray on the sideboard and pinned up a strand of hair which had escaped from her bun.

'As much as it ever is.' Dr Watson sat down heavily

in the basket-chair. 'This is the individual — who shot Holmes last night.'

'Oh!' Mrs Hudson's hand flew to her mouth.

'Just a nick,' Mr Holmes said. 'I imagine I might have done the same thing.'

'You see?' Dr Watson frowned. Mrs Hudson shook her head at Mr Holmes, smiling, and withdrew.

'Watson, help our visitor to a cup of tea, please.'

Dr Watson sighed, got up from his chair, and poured me a cup. 'Milk? Sugar?'

'Just milk, please.'

'Sugar's good for shock,' he replied, putting in two lumps. I grimaced as I drank, but presently started to feel a little better.

Sherlock Holmes fidgeted in his chair. 'To return to our subject, why have you come, J —' A comical expression flitted over his face. 'I am not quite sure how to address you.'

'I go by the name of Jack Hargreaves,' I said, firmly.

The corner of his mouth twisted up. 'Very well, Jack Hargreaves. Tell us your errand.'

'I — well — it's hard to know where to begin.'

'Try the beginning.' His voice was a gun wrapped in velvet.

I met his gimlet eyes and blushed. 'I answered an advertisement for a personal assistant. It gave no hint of what business I would be engaged in.'

'And you were a clerk previously.'

I stared. 'How do you..?'

'An educated guess,' said Mr Holmes. 'What made you change your situation?'

'I would prefer not to say.'

'Personal difficulties?'

'If you like, yes.'

'And now you are in over your head.'

'Yes! I've never stolen anything. I had never shot a gun before yesterday.'

'I could tell,' remarked Mr Holmes.

'I thought of running away, but — if it was just stealing I could understand that. But it's stealing to order for someone, and not normal things, not money or jewellery. And it isn't only Fingers, others are doing it too —'

'What are they stealing?'

'Fingers — Mr Molloy — said he stole metals you would find in a laboratory. I probably don't know the half of it, but I don't like the sound of it.'

I could almost see Sherlock Holmes's brain flicking through possibilities like a card file. 'And he is directed by someone?'

I nodded. 'He takes what he's told to take, nothing more. Please —'

'Yes?'

'If you can let Fingers off, somehow . . . He's been kind to me, and he's out of his depth too, however much he'd swear he isn't.'

'We shall see what we can do.' Mr Holmes's eyes

locked on mine. 'Tell me, Jack, does the name Moriarty mean anything to you?'

'I don't know anyone called Moriarty.'

He looked at me for a long moment. 'And who directs Fingers' actions?'

I studied my boots. 'The person in charge is called Mr Robinson.'

Sherlock Holmes snorted. 'An alias, no doubt.' He stood and extended a hand. 'Well, Jack, you were right to come to me. I take it no-one knows where you are?'

'I hope not.' I stood and shook his firm, dry hand, wondering what to do next. Would they give me a room, or should I go to a hotel for the night?

'Excellent.' He consulted his watch. 'Well, you had better hurry back. We don't want any awkward —'

'Go back?' I faltered. 'But I —'

'You have brought us some useful information, Jack Hargreaves, but I suspect there is much more to learn. You are just the person to learn it, and report back to me. Come, I shall accompany you home — at a discreet distance, of course. I would like to know where Fingers Molloy lays his head.'

I sensed Sherlock Holmes's presence in the shadows as I walked back to Upper Wimpole Street. I thought of making a run for it — but it would be no use. I was caught like a fly in a web, and now I had to go back into a situation which made my flesh crawl. And mixed up in it all, ringing round my head, was a question I chose not to answer: *Why didn't you tell them his name?*

Chapter 10

On Tenterhooks

I confess with no shame that I clock-watched throughout Holmes's absence. Not because I feared for his safety; my eagerness for his return was driven entirely by curiosity. I would burst with questions if he were not back soon.

An hour after his departure a key scraped in the lock. I rushed onto the first-floor landing, from which I observed Holmes removing his hat and peeling off his gloves. 'Well, come on, man!'

Holmes chuckled. 'You have some mild interest in my outing then, Watson. We can discuss it over dinner.'

'But that's not till seven!'

'Patience is a virtue, Watson.' Holmes shrugged off his coat. 'I have a few messages to send, and some light reading to keep me occupied.'

'You might tell me something,' I grumbled.

'Fear not, Watson, all will be revealed — such as it is — in good time.' Holmes's eyes twinkled, but he would not be persuaded.

Holmes came to the sitting room shortly afterwards and scribbled a note at the bureau. He folded it and wrote another, pausing every so often as if in a brown study. He rang the bell and handed the notes to Billy. 'Both to go as telegrams — this to Inspector Gregson, this to Professor MacTaggart. The addresses are included. Fast as you can and there's a shilling in it for you.' Billy took the notes and vanished.

'Isn't that —'

'Yes,' said Holmes. He went to the bookcase and extracted two large volumes. Then he crossed to the sensation fiction and penny dreadfuls; but when he caught my watching eye he returned to the bureau.

'You can trust me, Holmes.' I remarked, somewhat nettled.

'Implicitly, Watson. But I do not want you to jump to conclusions.'

The next hour was one of the longest of my life. I knew better than to interrupt Holmes; but I fretted and fidgeted until he raised his head and said, 'Would you mind going for a walk, old chap?'

'I might as well,' I snapped, and banged the door behind me.

The evening air cooled me a little, but inside I was still rubbed raw. I was Holmes's confidante and biographer; I had, to a great extent, made him famous. And yet he would not let me into his secrets! The busy streets jangled my nerves and I repaired to Regent's Park. Yet peace eluded me there too; young couples were giggling and whispering on the seats set furthest from the lamps, and the sound infuriated me. Had silence gone from the world entirely?

I returned to Baker Street at five minutes to seven, and tugged the door-bell. Holmes had had his time, and now it was mine.

Holmes was lying on the settee reading a penny dreadful, which he stuffed under a cushion when he saw me. 'Hullo, Watson, did you have a pleasant stroll?'

'Not especially.' I poured myself a small glass of whisky. 'I take it dinner will arrive shortly.'

'I expect so,' said Holmes, smiling. I took refuge in the newspaper.

Dinner was a fried sole with boiled potatoes, carrots, and a shrimp sauce. It was one of my favourites, but tonight I pushed it around my plate.

Holmes made a hearty meal, and pushed his knife and fork exactly together. 'There is no need for jealousy, Watson.'

'I beg your pardon?'

'You are angry with me, Watson. Firstly because I treated that young woman with what you perceive as undue leniency. Secondly' — Holmes began to tick the points off on his fingers — 'because I have sent her back into the field to spy for me, while keeping you in the dark. Thirdly, because you believe that means I trust her more than I do you. And fourthly, I suspect, because you worry she will lead me astray. Am I right?' He was smiling, but his gaze was steady, and uncomfortably penetrating.

I shifted in my chair. 'I wouldn't have put it quite like that…' Damn Holmes's deductive powers!

'Perhaps not.'

I felt myself growing warmer. 'Perhaps if you explained some of it to me —'

'I shall, while you make another attempt on that poor fish. I hope you operate on your patients with a little more finesse.' I poured another glass of wine and took up my fork, and Holmes continued. 'Consider, Watson, if we had delivered Jack straight to Lestrade. He would have interrogated her, gone straight to Fingers Molloy's residence, and arrested everyone. I have a strong suspicion Fingers Molloy knows better than to spill the beans about what is going on — if he knows enough to spill any beans. An additional factor is that Fingers and Co are installed in a fancy townhouse. There is money behind this operation, Watson.' Holmes's face was solemn.

'Is that why you've wired Gregson and not Lestrade?'

'Precisely. You are a fast learner.' Holmes sipped his wine. 'I have asked Gregson to put a plain-clothes man nearby, and I may supplement him with an Irregular if it seems worthwhile. Point two. I have sent Jack back in because, though we know a great deal more than we did yesterday, there is clearly much more to it. Fingers Molloy trusted Jack enough to require her assistance in a tight spot, and I trust her to keep herself out of any serious trouble. I suspect mild deception is the limit of her villainy, and we shall use that to our advantage.'

'And point four?' Holmes raised his eyebrows. 'The leading astray?'

'Oh!' He laughed. 'If I favoured women in breeches, Watson, I could find those at the music hall. I think I am safe enough.' He paused. 'Although I am sure she would cut a handsome figure in a dress.'

'Holmes —' He shook with laughter and I frowned. 'That was unfair.'

'It was, rather. But I do not ask if you are likely to fall in love with your female patients.' Holmes sipped his wine. 'I perceive that you recognise the name MacTaggart.'

'The professor of the chemical laboratory at Barts? He was there when I studied.'

'Quite. I have requested a chat with him tomorrow at the laboratory. I do not intend to let anything slip, but I want to know what metals he keeps there; how much, and under what conditions. It is not a field I am expert in, but I have been reading up.' He waved a hand at the bureau.

'Will you warn him about Fingers Molloy?'

'Not yet. There are much bigger laboratories, which I imagine hold larger stocks. On which note, I shall ask Huggins to find reports of all break-ins at scientific institutes during the last few years.' He paused. 'Does that satisfy your thirst for knowledge?'

'The penny dreadful under the settee cushion..?'

'You are like a hound on the scent, Watson, worse than Lestrade.' Holmes produced a small, garish paperback, which he handed to me.

'"*The Fiendish Experiments of Doctor X*"' I read. The cover showed a villainous-looking character bent over a glowing test-tube. From it rose a vapour which assumed the form of a screaming woman. 'Holmes, you can't think —'

'Not literally, no.' Holmes twitched the book from my hand and replaced it on the shelf. 'But these writers are inventive, they have fertile imaginations, and they understand what people dread. I imagine a master criminal operates in much the same way.' He sat back down. 'And for now, Watson, we have done all we can. Would you accompany me tomorrow, if you can spare the time?'

I smiled. 'I would be delighted, Holmes. Shall I ring for coffee?'

Chapter 11

A Midnight Mission

'Where've you been?' Fingers Molloy demanded, glaring at me.

'For a walk.' I held out a copy of *The Times*. 'I bought a paper to make sure we're not in it.'

'Oh. Good.' Fingers took the paper, glanced at the front page, and gave it back to me. 'I was worried you'd been took up.'

'Come on, Fingers, I've been sneaking around for years!' I spoke with a rough jollity which I did not feel.

He chuckled. 'S'pose you have. Anyway, you're just in time for dinner. Snell's got some sausages on the go.'

I checked my watch. 'Isn't it a bit early?'

'Ah, well, we're making an evening call.' Fingers gave me a slow wink. 'Remember the paper Mr Smith gave me at the Gentleman's Retreat?'

'The one you burnt?'

'The very same. Tonight's the night, and it'll be a bit of a journey.'

'Not the time machine again...' My stomach turned over.

'Wouldn't be offering you dinner if it was!' grinned Fingers. 'This one's strictly in the here and now, but it's a long trip.'

'Where are we going?'

'We're visiting a friend's kitchen to borrow a few ingredients.' Fingers snorted at my puzzled face. 'All in good time, Jack. And speaking of time, hurry Snell along with those sausages. We've got a train to catch.'

Less than an hour later Fingers and I were squashed against other commuters in a swaying train carriage. I was excited and apprehensive in equal measure, and I still had no idea what we were going to do. 'You go in a different queue to me,' Fingers had said out of the side of his mouth, as the cab slowed and Paddington station came into view. 'Get a ticket to Oxford, and 'ere, pay in coin.' He gave me a handful of sovereigns and half-sovereigns. 'Go in the second carriage from the front.' I asked for my ticket in the deepest voice I could manage, my collar turned up and my hat well down, and was surprised not to be arrested on the spot.

Gradually the pressure of bodies in the carriage lessened as people disembarked, carrying briefcases and bags. Their workday was ending, and ours was about to begin. I had no luggage but Fingers had brought a smart leather briefcase of his own, which I assumed was not merely a prop. I remembered the skeleton key, and wondered what other ingenious things Fingers had up his sleeve.

All the lamps were lit when we arrived at our destination. 'Oxford . . . Oxford,' shouted the attendants, rapping on the windows. Fingers nodded, and we joined the crowd jostling along the platform.

Fingers glanced at the station clock. 'Still early. We'll go for a drink.'

'Is that wise?'

'It'll give you a bit of Dutch courage. Besides, you need something to keep the cold out.' Fingers strolled into the nearest tavern. 'Two brandies, please.' He handed one to me and knocked the other straight back. 'An' another for me. Come on, let's get a seat.' He led me to a bench in a dark corner, and plopped down next to a drooping aspidistra.

'Take it easy, Fingers,' I warned, sipping my brandy. The glow inside was pleasant, but I hoped I would not have to drag Fingers to a lodging house to sleep it off, or worse, be apprehended in a noisy break-in. Fingers grinned, and tipped his brandy into the aspidistra pot in one swift motion.

Several more brandies went the same way, with Fingers appearing more drunk as the evening went on. At a quarter to eleven he stood, announced 'I can't feel my feet!' to the bar, and collapsed on the floor. I managed to get my hands under his armpits and drag him to a sitting position, and he pulled himself up clinging to the table like a toddler learning to walk. 'Give us a hand, Jack me boy, I'm done.' He flung an arm round my shoulders, and we left the bar by a weaving path, to the jeers and laughter of the remaining drinkers.

We continued to weave as we progressed slowly along the street. 'Was that necessary?' I muttered.

Fingers broke off from the ballad he was singing. 'If something gets missed tomorrow, and the police go round asking questions, I don't want people remembering two strangers hanging around. A young student and his drunken old pal, that's a different matter. Ain't it?' He squeezed my shoulder gently. 'Now we'll 'ave a nice slow stroll, and when we arrive it'll be time to get to work.' His voice lifted in song again as a couple approached arm-in-arm, and they gave him a wide berth.

We were among the university colleges now, and I marvelled at the magnificent buildings looming above me. 'Not bad, eh?' said Fingers, steering me to the right. The streets were quietening now, and a chill ran through me as the brandy began to wear off. We passed the Ashmolean Museum, then St John's, and Fingers lurched down a passage by a tavern called the Lamb and Flag, pulling me with him. I jumped as a clock struck the half-hour. It was so quiet now that the thumping of my heart in my chest sounded loud as a drum.

We made a left turn, then a right, and Fingers steered me across a well-kept lawn. The shadows of Gothic arches loomed around us. Fingers took his arm away and drew a shaded torch from his pocket. 'Here it is.' The dim light showed a higgledy-piggledy building like a gingerbread house, all angles and chimneys and points. He handed me his case and strode forward, tool-roll in hand. 'This window's a good 'un.' He oiled the hinges, inserted a pick into the catch, and it swung open. 'Come on, Jack, nightwatchman'll be round in five minutes.' He put a leg over the sill and vanished. I followed, recalling Snell's question about fitness.

My heart skipped a beat when Fingers's breath tickled my ear. 'Got the case?'

'Yes. Where are we?'

'In a laboratory.'

'You said we were going to a kitchen!'

'Shhh! This is it. The Abbot's Kitchen.' He took the case from me and placed it on what I now recognised as a workbench. 'We'll keep it brief.' He had the skeleton key ready, and went straight to a cabinet in the corner. He shone the torch briefly, reached in, and drew out a glass jar two-thirds full of dull silvery balls. 'Get me an empty jar from the case, Jack.'

The catches gave silently. Inside, the case was fitted with compartments containing many small jars, held by leather straps. All but three were full of coloured beads, with cotton wool stuffed in the top to keep them from rattling.

'Thankee,' said Fingers, as I unscrewed the lid. 'Hold steady, now.' He poured a few of the silver balls into the jar, peered at it, and shook in a few more, packing cotton wool on top. 'All done.' He replaced the jar in the cabinet, locked it, and picked up the briefcase. 'We'll wait for the watchman to pass, and we'll be on our way.'

'That's it?' I felt as if I'd gone to a play and they'd missed off the last act. 'We came all this way for a few metal balls?'

'We did. Duck!' A beam of light raked the windows for an instant, and the nightwatchman's measured tread passed by. 'You'd be more impressed if you knew what it was we've just nicked.'

'Do *you* know?'

Fingers dug me in the ribs. 'Course I do! Proper valuable stuff this. Ooray . . . Ooray . . . anyway, it's got a big U on the label. Easy to pinch, too, not like some of the stuff Mr Smith asks for.' He peeped above the window-ledge. 'He's gone. Let's hook it.'

Five minutes later we were weaving along a main thoroughfare, and Fingers was singing again. 'Are we going back now?' I asked.

Fingers kept bawling till we were alone. 'There's another lab less than a mile away. As we've done so well, I reckon we should take a shot at it before we turn in for the night. I'd rather be doing a bit of honest work than sleeping under a hedge.' He paused. 'We can do that after, and get the early train back. *Sweet Molly, sweet Molly Maloooooonnnne...*' And we continued to stagger down the street together.

Chapter 12

Questions And Quackery

'Are you any wiser, Watson?' Holmes asked as we descended the laboratory steps.

I glanced across but he did not appear to be making fun of me. 'If anything, I am further in the dark now than when we went in.'

My memories of Professor MacTaggart recalled a waspish, irascible man. Far from mellowing with age, he had soured like a fine vinegar. He demanded to know *why* we were enquiring about the chemicals he kept, and to *what* use we intended to put the information. Holmes offered plausible explanations, which the professor dismissed with a wave of the hand. 'I don't know what you're up to, Mister Sherlock Holmes,' he growled, 'but you'll get no change out of me till you tell me what you're really here for.'

Holmes shrugged. 'Very well, Professor. I'm

investigating a time-travelling burglar who steals precious metals from chemical laboratories, and I want to know what he's doing with them.'

The professor's eyebrows shot into his white hair. 'So! And what is he taking?'

'My source is a little vague.'

'Precious metals aren't something we keep much of,' mused the professor. 'We generally use small quantities, and besides, there's the security risk. You can inspect what we do have, but our equipment is considerably more valuable than our stock of raw elements.'

'You have no fear of theft?'

The professor frowned at Holmes. 'Our premises are secure, and our staff vigilant.'

'I imagine most of the laboratories this man has robbed would say the same,' countered Holmes.

Unfortunately the professor took umbrage at this, and bustled us off shortly afterwards claiming he had a scientific paper to finish. The door banged behind us, and the key turned in the lock.

'Charming, wasn't he?' said Holmes.

'Sssh, he'll hear you!' I muttered.

'I don't care if he does. Let us drop in on Huggins at the Yard. I almost hope we discover that old fool has been hoodwinked out of his entire stock ten times over.'

However, it was not to be. Huggins, while much more personable than the Professor, could offer little help. 'We only hold records for London, sir,' he sighed. 'I recall an equipment theft at University College. Thirty microscopes. They were found under a tarpaulin in a church vestry a month later. I don't suppose it's of much use —'

'No, but it is fascinating,' remarked Holmes.

Huggins beamed. 'I'll keep hunting. If I find anything, shall I contact you, or alert Inspector Lestrade?'

'Oh, don't bother the Inspector,' Holmes said, patting Huggins on the shoulder. 'Thank you very much for your assistance. We must be getting on.' When I glanced back Huggins was gazing at us wistfully.

'Well, so much for that line of enquiry,' I said, as we walked along the Strand. 'What a waste of time!'

'Ah, we may profit from it yet.' Holmes picked a thread from his lapel. 'I suspect we shall have to wait for a communication from Jack.'

I snorted. 'In that case, I shall do something useful and go to my consulting rooms.'

I arrived at my practice in a mood to roll my sleeves up and cure all ills, to find nobody waiting, no calls to make, and a long afternoon ahead of me. The most exciting occurrence was a visit from a travelling salesman urging me to recommend something called 'Dr Beaumont's Health Elixir' to my patients. 'It's wonderful stuff,' he enthused. 'I take it every day, and I'm in the peak of health!'

'You look it,' I laughed, 'but I'm not convinced it's down to this elixir you're peddling.' The man was in considerably better condition than most of the people I saw in the street; his eyes were bright, his skin clear, and his manner had a refreshing vigour.

'Well, I'll leave you a bottle, and you can try it for yourself.' He reached into his Gladstone bag and produced an elaborately-labelled bottle filled with vivid red liquid.

'And how much will that be?' I enquired, not touching the bottle.

'A shilling in the shops, but to you not a penny,' he grinned, putting it on my desk. 'I'll be on my way now.' I heard a cheery whistle as he descended the stairs.

I settled to read the newspaper in the hope I would be diverted by some patients, but at the corner of my eye the bottle gleamed red. I put down the paper and examined the bottle. 'Derived from natural ingredients'. Ha! You could say the same of cocaine! I uncorked the bottle. The elixir had a pleasantly fruity aroma, and when I licked my finger it tasted of plum-pudding. 'A small spoonful once daily is all you need!', the label proclaimed.

We shall see. I poured a teaspoonful. If it were a genuine tonic, well, some of my patients did require a pick-me-up, and if it made them feel better, who was I to argue? The elixir had a delightfully warming effect, like brandy but without the kick of alcohol. I corked the bottle and made a note of the time of dosage.

I spent the rest of the afternoon flicking through the newspaper and musing. No patients came; but was that not a good thing? Better for the population of London to be healthy than to crowd to my door! Perhaps when I returned to Baker Street Holmes would have made a breakthrough, and I would be his chronicler once more. And Jack would go back to doing whatever she did before, and there would be no more time-travelling villains. Nice straightforward criminality; a cypher to crack, or a tunnel under a bank...

I woke with a start, and glanced at my watch. Half-past four! It was unusual for me to take a nap in the day, but I felt completely refreshed, not dull and sluggish as I often did on waking. The bottle winked at me from the desk, and on impulse I tucked it into my coat pocket. Holmes would scoff, no doubt, but he didn't have to know. I could keep it in my bedroom. I strode along the pavement in seven-league boots, full of the joy of life.

Chapter 13

A Steady Hand

We arrived back in London the next day, stiff and grimy, but safe. The second break-in, at an Oxford college, had gone as well as the first. Fingers had added some more Ooray to his little jar, and in another he had placed some snippets of a soft metal ribbon. They came from a vessel labelled *Th* and sealed with wax round the lid.

'What's the wax for?'

Fingers paused in his careful resealing of the vessel with a stick of wax and a tiny heat-lamp. 'This stuff, whatsis, Thursday I call it, it doesn't like water. Got to take care, 'cos it don't like heat either.' He switched off the heat-lamp and regarded his work. 'That should do it. Mr Smith's always glad to get a bit of Thursday.'

'What does he do with it?'

'Blamed if I know. I'm quite a regular at a few

establishments of scientific education, though. It must be useful stuff, for all it don't look like much.'

'How much of it do you think you've taken, since you started going into labs?'

Even in the dim light from Fingers' night-torch, I could see I had gone too far. 'You're a curious young person, Jack.' He picked up the sealing-wax and for a minute or two was intent on sealing his own jar of Thursday. When he spoke again his voice was soft against the silence. 'That's a tendency you should curb. If you don't want to get into trouble.' He stood the jar on the workbench and switched off the heat-lamp, and the room was too dark for me to make out his expression.

'Yes, Fingers,' I whispered.

'That's more like it.' Fingers stowed his roll, blew on the jar to cool it, and slotted it into the case. 'This watchman's a bit less regular in his visits, so keep your eyes and ears peeled.' His skeleton key gleamed in the light from the gas lamp outside.

We were quiet after that. Fingers had said his piece, and I was exhausted and, I admit, distressed by the night's events. Fingers guided us to a meadow on the opposite side of the River Thames, and we sheltered behind a high hedge. I slept fitfully, starting awake from vivid dreams of being chased through a dark city and jerked backwards into nothingness by a hand clutching my shoulder. Dawn broke, and I was as tired as I had been when I lay down. Hot coffee and rolls at the station revived me, but I was still desperately low in spirits. I took refuge in a yellowback novel on the train, losing myself in another's adventures.

'We have a visitor!' boomed Mr Snell as we let ourselves in. 'Mr Smith has called again regarding the safe.'

'I have!' Mr Smith cried from the parlour, and presently walked into the hall balancing a cup of tea and a slice of plum-cake. 'And this time I have remembered to bring everything with me.'

'Just the man I was after,' said Fingers, putting his case on the hall table and opening the catches. 'A couple of items for you. Bit of Ooray, bit o' Thursday.'

'Perfect,' said Mr Smith, handing his crockery to Mr Snell. He took the jars and peered at their contents. 'I'll pass these to Mr Robinson without delay,' he said, putting the jars in his inner jacket pocket. 'I take it all went well?'

'Like clockwork, sir,' said Fingers. 'Jack's a steady hand.' For a moment his eyes said *You'd better be*.

'Jolly good.' Mr Smith rubbed his hands. 'Will you pop downstairs with me, Jack?'

'Of course.' I followed him to the basement, wishing I could at least have washed my face. Even my teeth felt gritty.

'Now . . . here we are.' Mr Smith found the knot in the panelling and the safe was revealed. He put a pair of kid gloves on and took the notebook with transparent pages from his pocket. 'No shakes today, Jack.' He smiled. 'Remember your steady hand.'

I wiped my hands on my handkerchief, made thumbs-up, and the deed was done. Mr Smith sliced the celluloid sheets out with his penknife. 'Could you take off my glove?' He extended his hand and his wrist was warm as I peeled the glove back. He opened the safe with his naked thumb and placed the celluloid sheets into two slots in the back of the door. 'Try it,' he said, closing the safe. I put my thumb on the metal disc and the door opened. He laughed as I examined my thumb. 'And the other one, Jack.' His voice lingered on my name, and the door unlocked again.

'Excellent,' said Mr Smith. 'Have you given any thought to that other matter, Jack?' His voice was casual, but his eyes were not.

'The opportunity?' He nodded. 'I . . . perhaps if I knew more about what was involved.'

He laughed, and moved a little closer. 'Well, it's a little hard to discuss with your current employer lurking above stairs. Perhaps you could slip out and meet me at the Gentleman's Retreat.'

'I — I'm not sure I remember the tune to get in,' I muttered. A runnel of sweat trickled down my back.

He put his mouth to my ear. 'I'll ask Jameson to watch for you. And I'll teach you the tune again, so you won't ever forget it.' He put his hand on my waist.

'I'll enjoy that.' His breath caressed my neck and he kissed me where my pulse beat. He murmured against my skin, 'Say four o'clock tomorrow?'

I nodded, full of shivers and unable to speak. I wanted him to kiss me again, there, everywhere. But he stepped back. 'You're shaking again, Jack,' he said, with amusement in his voice. 'You must learn to control it.' His bright brown eyes twinkled. 'Till tomorrow.'

I leaned against the wall while Mr Smith sauntered away. I realised I was panting for breath and loosened my necktie. What excuse could I make to leave the house tomorrow? And what on earth was I going to do? The panelling swam in front of my eyes, and I sat on the floor with a bump. *You can fall a lot further than this*, I thought, and that didn't help at all, because the next image was of being caught by Mr Smith's warm hands. Mr Smith. I didn't even know his first name, or if Mr Smith was his real name. And he wouldn't tell me anything until he got me in the Gentleman's Retreat, alone… My skin tingled. But a voice in my head, a rational, reasonable voice, was saying *You won't come back. Once you go, you won't come back.*

'You all right, Jack?' Fingers shouted.

'Yes.' I struggled to my feet and hauled myself upstairs. 'I'm going to have a bath.' It would give me time to cool off, time alone. But as I sponged myself I imagined Mr Smith watching, and grew hot all over again.

But it's wrong, stealing is wrong…

I scrubbed my skin with a towel, trying to scrub the little voice away. A victimless crime, Fingers had said. And Mr Smith was being kind to me…

Once you go, you won't come back.

Back in my bedroom I drew my suitcase from under the bed, and rummaged inside. I kept writing paper and envelopes for job applications, and I was glad of them now. My heart thumped, though my bedroom door was locked. I scribbled a few lines, sealed the envelope, and found a stamp. Pulling my dressing gown close about me, I opened the window. A small boy loitered outside. 'Hey!' I called softly. He squinted at me. 'Post this for me and I'll give you a penny!'

'Tuppence!'

I sighed. 'All right.' He caught the letter and I sent the coins after it. He touched his hat and strolled away, whistling.

What if Fingers or Snell had heard me? What if the boy didn't post the letter? I lowered the sash, closed the curtains, and began to dress. I had done what I could, and I told myself that it was out of my hands now. I tried to push the little voice down as I bandaged my chest, pulled on my trousers and tucked in my shirt, but it wouldn't go away, no matter how tightly I muffled it.

Chapter 14

Action Stations

'Thank goodness you're back, sir!' Billy scampered up the kitchen stairs to me. 'Mr Holmes has been beside himself!'

'What do you mean? I told him I would be at my consulting-room this afternoon, and I am not after my usual time.'

'It's not that, sir. A letter came an hour ago and he jumped for joy — actually jumped — and shouted "Where's Watson when I need him, eh?"'

'I'd better go to him, then.' I mounted the steps wondering what mood I should find Holmes in at the top.

'Watson, at last!'

'What's happened?'

'A communication from the field!' He waved a letter.

'There's no signature.'

'Oh Watson, look at the penmanship! It's from Jack!' He read:

'"*Oxford last night, took small amounts of metals U (Ooray) and Th (Thursday). Invited solo to London club tomorrow 4pm to learn more. Seek guidance.*" How's your chemistry, Watson?'

'Rusty —'

'They've been stealing uranium and thorium! Jack must have spotted the chemical symbols in the lab.'

My head felt foggy. 'So they've been to Oxford, and . . . what do uranium and thorium do?'

'Not much!' grinned Holmes. 'Uranium is used in stained glass, thorium in the new gas mantles.' He tapped the large volume sitting beside him on the settee.

'You seem very pleased about it.'

'Don't you see, Watson? We are dealing with a scientist! He must have found a new application for these elements, since they have little intrinsic value —' The door-bell jangled violently. 'Ah, Lestrade and Huggins are here.'

'But yesterday you were keeping Lestrade out of the case!'

'That was yesterday. Today is different, and there is no time to lose.' Holmes opened the sitting room door and shouted 'Come on up.'

Footsteps clattered and presently Lestrade appeared in the doorway, with Huggins peeping over his shoulder. 'I hope this is urgent, Holmes, I've left a report half-written.'

'We've tracked down your two favourite time-travellers, Lestrade.'

Lestrade's lip curled. 'The best news I've had all day. Can we arrest them now?'

'Not quite yet. It isn't normal pilfering — there's something much bigger going on, and we'll need help to crack it.'

'Organised crime?'

'*Scientific crime.*'

Lestrade raised his eyebrows. 'I have no idea what you mean.'

'Neither do I as yet. But I suspect we shall be much further on by tomorrow.'

'And what do you need me for, sir?' Huggins's voice was timid. 'I'm not really an arresting sort of person.'

'No, Huggins, your skills are much more specialised. I want you to do some research at the British Museum.'

'It won't be open now,' Huggins said, nervously.

'I shall telegraph a Librarian of my acquaintance who lives nearby and tell him to expect you outside within the hour. Here is your quarry.' Holmes passed him a sheet of paper. 'Do you have a notebook?'

'I always have a notebook.' Huggins patted his jacket pocket.

'Excellent. Wire me anything you find.' Huggins nodded and ran downstairs as though his life depended on it.

'Lestrade, I propose we strike while the iron is hot. A plain-clothes man is already on duty at the location, and I daresay we can round up a few more constables on the way. We want speed and numbers on this occasion. It shouldn't be difficult, but . . . I prefer to be sure.' Holmes looked troubled for an instant. 'Watson, take your gun, and I shall do the same.'

I went to my bedroom and fetched the gun, taking the opportunity to stow Dr Beaumont's Health Elixir at the bottom of my wardrobe. When I returned Holmes was writing at the bureau. 'Billy can take it to the telegraph-office,' he said. 'Lestrade, I don't suppose you came armed?'

'I always bring a revolver for urgent matters.' Lestrade opened his jacket, showing the holster at his side.

'Then we are ready.'

As we walked along Baker Street Holmes hailed a passing policeman, who fell in with us. 'It's quiet tonight,' he said grimly. 'I'd welcome a bit of action.'

'Have you any idea where your colleagues are walking?'

The policeman continued his slow tread as he considered. 'You'll find a bobby on Oxford Street for sure.'

'How far are we going?' asked Lestrade. 'I didn't expect to spent the night collecting policemen.'

'That's the best of it,' said Holmes. 'He is in Upper

Wimpole Street. He was under our noses all along.'

Lestrade's nose wrinkled. 'The cheeky swine!'

By the time we turned into Harley Street we had recruited two more helpers. 'Here's the plan,' said Holmes. 'The plain-clothes man knocks at the front door. Watson, another policeman and I stand ready to rush in. If the door isn't opened within a minute, we kick it in. Lestrade, you and the others charge the kitchen door. We apprehend first, ask questions later. Does that seem reasonable to you, Lestrade?'

'Exactly what I would have suggested, Holmes,' said Lestrade, drily.

'Let us adjust our watches.' We stood in a circle. 'At half past six, we make the move.'

A few minutes later Lestrade's team were in position on the area steps, Holmes had briefed the plain-clothes man, and we were loitering on the street corner. 'Ready, Watson?' whispered Holmes.

'Ready.' I touched the cool metal of the gun in my pocket.

'Then it is time.'

The plain-clothes policeman strode down the street, and we fell in behind him. He rapped on the front door.

The moment stretched. A tiny click, and the door began to move.

We surged forward, almost knocking down the old man in the hall, and the plain-clothes man took him by the arm. 'Go forward!' he cried, kicking the door closed. 'Now, come quietly,' he said to the trembling man, leading him to the parlour.

Something crashed beneath us. 'Lestrade's in!' cried Holmes. We ranged through the rooms on the ground floor. Jack was standing by the sitting-room window, pale but composed. She flinched when she saw us. 'I don't need to arrest you, do I?' said Holmes.

She bit her lip, and shook her head. 'He's downstairs,' she muttered. 'There's no-one else.'

We found Lestrade and his men in a long corridor. 'The doors are locked!'

'Barge them!' cried Holmes, and suited the action to the word. Lestrade and his companion charged the right hand door, and I ran to the end. The door gave easily, and I heard a little moan as I fell into the room. Fingers Molloy put his hands up. 'Don't shoot!'

'You're under arrest!'

'I know!' He was trembling like a leaf about to fall.

'Is he there?' Lestrade shouted from the corridor.

'Yes,' I cried over my shoulder.

'I — I'm a bit shook up,' said Fingers. 'Would you mind if I sat down?'

I motioned with my gun. He lowered himself into the easy chair, hands raised, eyes fixed on me. Then he twisted to his left.

'Stop or I shoot!' I yelled.

A cloth fell, and the time machine was revealed.

I acted on instinct. And my aim was true.

***

After the shot rang out, silence rose with the smoke. Then footsteps thumped along the corridor, and I heard Lestrade shouting. But my eyes were fixed on what I had done. My gun clunked on the floor, far away.

At the edge of my vision Fingers Molloy, his hands still raised, stood up. His mouth dropped open as he too stared at the time machine, shot right through the centre of its dial.

Chapter 15
Around The Table

My shame grew greater with every step. I had betrayed Fingers Molloy who had, in his own way, been kind to me. Depending on what Fingers told the police, I had also betrayed Mr Smith. And for what? A mere suspicion that something wasn't right, that this was more than common thieving. I hoped against hope that Mr Smith would get away and start afresh, out of Mr Robinson's employment. Perhaps I could join him . . . but I dashed that aside.

The voices were coming from the dining room. I pushed the door open and all eyes turned to me. Fingers was sitting at the table, his cuffed hands resting on the cloth. Sherlock Holmes was on one side of him, and on the other was the policeman who had been at the Jewel House. Dr Watson was guarding Mr Snell, who, also handcuffed, sat upright and silent. Two other policemen stood by.

'So,' said Fingers. 'It was you.' He was half-smiling, but the gleam in his eyes was far from amusement.

'I'm sorry, Fingers.' I twisted my hands.

The policeman sitting by him frowned. '*You* shopped Fingers?'

'She did, Inspector Lestrade,' said Dr Watson.

'*She?*' exclaimed the Inspector, staring at me. I itched to turn away, but I suspected that might lead to an arrest.

'Some detective *you* are,' muttered Fingers.

'Lestrade.' The policeman turned towards Sherlock Holmes. 'Don't gawp. It's impertinent.'

Lestrade blushed. 'Sorry, but I didn't —'

'You did the right thing, Jack. Take a seat.' Mr Holmes addressed the policeman. 'Jack came to Baker Street with — misgivings about the nature of her employment. Much is still unclear, but we are now in a position to go forward.' His eyes settled on Fingers.

'I'm saying nothing,' muttered Fingers, a mutinous expression on his face.

'Is that wise, Fingers?' Sherlock Holmes's eyes glinted. 'Coutts Bank, the Aston affair, an attempt on the Crown Jewels, and now stealing from laboratories. Any one of those would put you away for years.'

Fingers sighed. 'Awright.' He shifted in his chair. 'If I do let the cat out of the bag, what's in it for me?'

'A reduced sentence,' said Inspector Lestrade.

'A pardon, if you keep your nose clean,' said Mr Holmes.

'What?' Lestrade leaned round Fingers to stare at the detective.

'You're doing it again, Lestrade. Now, Fingers, the whole story. Who you're working for, the jobs you've done, where you got the time machine. I want everything laid on this table in exchange for a clean sheet. Do we have a deal?'

Fingers's eyes shone like a weasel's on spying a plump young mouse. 'Take the cuffs off me and Snell, and yes, we do.'

The next hour was an education. I was sent, with a police guard, to fetch the tools of Fingers's trade. He demonstrated the skeleton key, the heat lamp, the night-torch and many more devices, and the policemen exclaimed over them. Everyone gathered round him in the corridor as he opened the safe with his thumb. The Inspector filled pages of his notebook, and had to ask for a pencil when his pen ran dry. Fingers described his many robberies; how he had got in, and how he had got out again, down to the Oxford job we had performed less than a day before. His eyes twinkled as he held court and the audience gasped.

'And your patron, Fingers,' said Mr Holmes, when Fingers finally paused for breath.

'The man at the top of the tree?' Fingers's eyes darted to me and back. 'He's called Mr Robinson.'

'What sort of man is he?'

'I can't exactly say, as I've never met him.'

'Remember your bargain, Fingers Molloy.'

'I'm telling the truth! I only know his name!'

'Cuff him,' Lestrade said to the two waiting policemen.

'No!' Fingers raised his hands in surrender. 'The man I deal with is called Mr Smith. But he just does what he's told, same as me! He just answers to Robinson!'

'Step back,' Sherlock Holmes told the policemen. 'Jack, the meeting you mentioned tomorrow at a club . . . is it with Mr Smith?'

'What meeting?' asked Fingers.

I studied the threads in the tablecloth. 'Mr Smith invited me to the Gentleman's Retreat tomorrow afternoon to . . . explain a few things.'

'Oh, really.' Fingers grinned. 'Watch yourself, Jack, he wants to get into yer breeches. I've seen how he looks at you.'

I couldn't raise my head; I knew they were all staring at me from the way my face burned. At that moment, if the ground had opened and swallowed me, I would have thanked it.

'Mr Molloy!' scolded Mr Snell.

'This Mr Smith,' said Sherlock Holmes, slowly, 'he isn't a tall man with a high forehead and deep-set eyes, is he?'

Fingers laughed. 'The exact opposite! He's a plump little cove, our Mr Smith.'

Mr Holmes sighed. 'I don't suppose the name Moriarty means anything to you?'

'Nah.'

'Your pet theory is exploded, Holmes,' Lestrade remarked.

'Unless the mysterious Mr Robinson... Ha!' Sherlock Holmes made a peculiar little shaking movement. 'Well, we shall see. This Gentleman's Retreat you speak of, is it far away?'

'Just off Charing Cross Road.' I heard myself say.

'Excellent. I have the beginnings of a plan forming in my mind,' Sherlock Holmes announced to the room. 'But first I should like a private word with Jack. May we use your sitting room, Fingers?'

Fingers shrugged. 'It's not like I can stop you.'

Sherlock Holmes did not speak till we were seated facing each other, alone. 'Mr Fingers Molloy has touched a nerve, I perceive.'

I scarcely managed a nod.

'Could you meet Mr Smith tomorrow, as planned?'

I tried to swallow the lump in my throat. 'What will happen if I do?'

'It depends.' Mr Holmes ran his long fingers down the arm of his chair. 'A few of us will be standing ready nearby, charming as Mr Smith undoubtedly is.'

'How do you know?' I asked, startled.

Mr Holmes smiled. 'Well, you never mentioned Mr Smith to me at all, and Fingers wouldn't say his name until Lestrade threatened him with the cuffs.

The man must have something going for him.'

'Will you arrest him?' My heart felt as if someone was squeezing it tight.

'We'll see. But remember why you came to us, Jack. You suspected something big. Meeting Mr Smith is the only way to learn more.' He paused. 'We could, perhaps, offer him a pardon in exchange for information about this Mr Robinson, as we have done with Fingers.'

The grip on my heart relaxed. 'I'll meet him.' I said. 'But if you could find a way not to arrest him —'

'I shall do what I can.' Sherlock Holmes stood up. 'We should rejoin the others. Thank you for your help, Jack. And one last thing…'

I stood too. 'What is it?'

'Do be careful.'

Chapter 16
A Very Busy Man

Holmes's laughter rang out all the way upstairs. 'Well!' he exclaimed, flinging open the sitting-room door. 'Let me get out of these togs, Watson, and I shall tell all.' He was attired as a vicar, sporting a pair of enormous muttonchops. Five minutes later he reappeared as himself, took up his pipe, and reached for the Persian slipper. I lowered my paper in anticipation.

'I'm waiting, Holmes,' I reminded him, after a few minutes of silent pipe-smoking.

'The Gentleman's Retreat is a remarkable place.' Holmes took another puff. 'I could not loiter, but from what I have managed to observe it is like an iceberg. A ramshackle little joint on the surface, but massive beneath.' He pointed at his walking stick with the pipe. 'At a guess it is the size of a ballroom, for the pavement rings hollow several yards before and after the front door. There is no back door. No visible back door, anyway.'

'Do you suspect the back door of being invisible?' I laughed.

Holmes grinned back. 'I wouldn't put it past the ingenious mind we are dealing with. I suspect it is either camouflaged to perfection, or much further away than your average back door. I rambled about the neighbourhood, but I could not discover it.'

'The plan is still on?'

'Oh yes.' Holmes lay back on the settee and blew smoke rings. 'I would dearly love to know what is down there. It will be difficult to restrain Lestrade from breaking and entering, for I am as curious as he.'

The door-bell pealed and we both started. Words were exchanged, and light footsteps ran upstairs. *A telegram.*

A knock sounded. 'Come in, Billy,' Holmes snapped.

'I — I'm sorry to disturb you...' Huggins peeped round the door.

'Huggins!' Holmes cried. 'Sit down, sit down.' He sprang up and plumped the cushions on the basket-chair. 'Have you been at the British Museum all these hours?'

'I like to be thorough.' Huggins perched on the extreme edge of the chair. 'When I finished, I decided it was quicker to get a cab and tell you than to explain it all in a telegram.' He drew out his notebook. 'I did as you asked, sir. All the scientific journals for the last fifteen years, and any articles concerning uranium, thorium, or both. I feel quite an expert.'

'I am sure you do,' said Holmes. 'I take it you found something?'

'I did, sir. I started from the most recent material and worked back. Relevant papers from the last few years were mainly overviews or summaries of earlier research. Then I found a scientific paper from five years ago discussing potential applications of uranium, based on the authors' earlier discovery that it emitted some form of light rays.' Huggins paused. 'I apologise, Mr Holmes, I am not much of a scientist —'

'This is wonderful, Huggins. Did you manage to find any related papers?'

'Yes, two. One described the experiments leading to the discovery of the rays — that was two years before — and a paper a year after outlined the possibility of...' Huggins frowned at his notebook, 'further actinides.'

'And the authors?'

'Each paper was written by a team of scholars at the University of Oxford. The names differed slightly for each article — probably due to a change in staff — but one name was listed in all three.'

'Go on,' Holmes and I were also on the edges of our seats now.

'Mr T.J. Smith.'

'No!' I exclaimed.

'It appears that our Mr Smith is a very busy man,' Holmes said, drily.

'Not after the last article, he wasn't,' said Huggins. 'I checked the most recent journals again, but he was missing.'

'Probably because he's been working on those further applications all by himself.' Holmes's jaw clenched.

'Maybe,' said Huggins. 'His name was well down the list in all three papers. Wouldn't that mean he was a junior staff member, or even a student?'

'It's a good point, Huggins, but I am inclined to have a high estimation of Mr T.J. Smith. Was there anything else?'

'Nothing so relevant. I made a list, though.' Huggins tore out a page and passed it to Holmes.

'You have done sterling work, Huggins. This will help us tremendously in the afternoon's expedition. Speaking of which, we should make our way to Upper Wimpole Street and brief Lestrade before he goes in with both feet. Watson, get your gun. Oh, and muffle yourself. When we get near the Gentleman's Retreat I expect eyes everywhere. What is it, Huggins?' Huggins had half-raised a hand.

'Could I come, sir?' His eyes were shining. 'I've never been on an expedition.'

'Can you handle a gun?'

'Yes, sir,' said Huggins, a trifle indignantly.

'Very well, so long as you keep to the rear and do as you're told. Extra hands are always welcome.' Holmes disappeared into his room and emerged with a thick woollen scarf, which he handed to Huggins. 'Your own coat and hat will do.'

I was reaching into my wardrobe for a wide-brimmed hat when my eye caught the little bottle sitting on the floor. A little early, but — it would perk me up. I uncorked the bottle and drank a little, and the familiar warmth coursed through me. I checked my gun, put on my hat, and strode into the sitting room.

'What's that on your tie?' Holmes narrowed his eyes.

A trickle of red was running down the lilac silk. 'I'll go and change it.'

'But what is it?'

Curse Holmes's observational skills! 'Just a tonic I've been taking.'

'A tonic? You, Watson, of all people, indulging in quackery!'

'Holmes, I'm a doctor. I tried it in a spirit of investigation, and I believe it does me good.'

'Fetch the bottle.' I sighed, and complied. '"Dr Beaumont's Health Elixir,"' Holmes read. 'Ha!' He thrust my discarded newspaper under my nose. An attractive young woman beamed from an advertisement. *Dr Beaumont's Health Elixir, for that Inner Glow!*

Holmes examined the bottle. 'No ingredients. You should pour it down the sink where it belongs.'

I snatched the bottle back. 'It does me good!' The words rang out much louder than I had intended.

'Put it down, Watson.' Holmes's voice was hard and cold. 'I shall analyse your "tonic" when I have less pressing things to do.' Huggins was staring at me with eyes as round as buttons. 'Come along, you two,' said Holmes, and his tone was softer. 'Now we know what we are dealing with, Jack needs us more than ever.'

Chapter 17
La Fée Verte

An observer would have thought I had not a care in the world as I sauntered along Charing Cross Road. I had my best suit on, my shoes were polished, and I wore a carnation in my buttonhole. But inside I was far from carefree.

I had barely slept the previous night, tired though I was. When I did close my eyes I dreamt of being chased up and down stairs by a gang of policemen, spilling a trail of beads as I ran. Inspector Lestrade had ordered three of the policemen to watch us overnight, and their steady tread had doubtless contributed to my nightmares.

The Inspector arrived in the early afternoon, and Sherlock Holmes and Dr Watson were not far behind. They had brought with them a tall, skinny young man. 'Huggins!' exclaimed Lestrade. 'What are you doing here?'

'He's come along to join the fun,' said Mr Holmes. 'Don't worry, I'll mind him.' He reached into his pocket. 'Jack, I have something for you.' He handed me a tiny silver whistle. 'One of my own gadgets; try it. Gently!' he cried. I breathed into the whistle. It shrieked like a banshee and everyone covered their ears. 'If you want us, use it. One of us will always be near. I only hope the cellar is not too deep for us to hear you. In fact, if you are not back within the hour, we will break in.'

'No need for that,' said Fingers. 'The door works on a little tune.' He whistled five notes. 'Your go.' He whistled the notes again, over and over, until the whole room, policemen, detectives, and thieves, whistled in unison. 'We're meant to wait for the squeezebox man, but this works just as well.'

'Excellent,' said Mr Holmes. 'Jack, make yourself ready, and bring a gun.'

As I turned into the alley the accordion player was nowhere to be seen. I put my hands in my pockets, and the little whistle was cool to the touch. I remembered Sherlock Holmes's last words to me, 'Jack, if you are in danger, or uneasy, or even uncomfortable, use the whistle. Don't wait too long.'

The door to the Gentleman's Retreat swung open and Jameson, minus his goggles, beckoned me in. This time the stairwell was lit. I pushed open the door at the foot of the stairs and there, sitting alone at a table, was Mr Smith.

He stood as I entered. 'Welcome! Come and have a drink. Jameson, two of the usual. Is all secure?'

'It is, sir.'

'Take yourself off for an hour or two, then.' Jameson raised his eyebrows, and presently glasses clinked at the bar.

Mr Smith smiled at me. 'After our drink, I shall give you the grand tour. Unless you have something else in mind?'

'Oh no, that sounds — that sounds good,' I stammered. *A grand tour? Of where?*

'Your drinks,' I jumped at Jameson's voice. His tray held two glasses, each with a measure of green liquor, a jug of iced water, and a bowl of sugar lumps. On each glass rested a silver spoon like filigree.

'Thank you, Jameson.' Mr Smith watched him out of the door. 'La Fée Verte. Can I help you to sugar?'

'No, thank you.' Mr Smith put a sugar lump on his spoon and poured water onto it. The green liquor began to pale and cloud. 'What is it?'

'The green fairy. Absinthe.' He put the jug down. 'You should dilute it well if it's your first time.'

I filled the small glass with water, concentrating on keeping a steady hand. Mr Smith's eyes twinkled over the rim of his glass. 'Go on.' I took a sip, and tried not to make a face. It tasted of nasty medicine.

He laughed. 'It's an acquired taste.' I tried another sip but it was no better. The taste wound into me like ivy. It crept into my blood and made it run cold.

Mr Smith drained his glass. 'I have a present for you.' He took my hand and I let him guide me across the room. He reached behind one of the gilded mirrors and a panel pivoted, revealing a plain corridor.

'I had to guess a few things. I hope I got it right.' Mr Smith opened the first door. He appeared more excited than I had ever seen him. 'I'll wait outside.'

I did not let my expression slip until I had pulled the door closed. On a tailor's dummy hung a low-cut sleeveless dress of emerald silk, and underneath stood a pair of high-heeled boots. I opened the tallboy to find stockings, petticoats, underwear, a corset and a bustle. On top of the tallboy was a long velvet box, and inside was the diamond and emerald necklace which Fingers had given Mr Smith at our first meeting. Another box held diamond ear-rings with screws. Next to it lay a false plait of hair, and a packet of pins.

So this was what he wanted, said the little voice. I put a hand on the tallboy to steady myself. Don't wait too long, Mr Holmes had said. But I could not blow the whistle. I had uncovered nothing except that Mr Smith wanted me to dress as a woman. And I had to carry on, or I would fail everyone I had pulled into this.

Ten minutes later I was more uncomfortable than I had ever been, physically and mentally. I had never worn anything more complicated than a maid's dress, and the corset bit into me, the bustle and petticoats dragged me down, the ear-rings pinched, the hairpins pulled. I thrust the whistle into my bodice. There was nowhere to hide the gun; no room in the boots, no breathing-space in the clothes, no pockets.

Mr Smith beamed when I opened the door. 'You are beautiful, my dear. La Fée Verte, indeed. And what is your given name? Jack will hardly do for this fine lady.' He took my arm. He was feverishly warm beneath his shirt.

'Mary,' I lied. I would not have told him my real name for anything.

His face fell a little. 'I had expected something more exotic for a woman like you. Daring, spirited... I shall name you Esmeralda. Yes.' He stroked my cheek with his forefinger. 'I'll show you the workshop.'

I wobbled along on Mr Smith's arm, the train of the dress slithering behind me. The next room had a large workbench in the middle, lit by a low, wide lamp. One wall was made of small drawers, each with a neat white label. Otherwise it was completely bare. 'This is where the devices take shape.' He pulled out a drawer full of tiny screws.

'Like the skeleton key?'

'That's right.' He pushed the drawer closed. 'But there's more to see.'

The next room was a laboratory, again pristine and empty. The shelves were stacked with jars, and I saw one marked *U*, much bigger than the one in the Abbot's Kitchen. 'Isn't that what Fingers and I took?' I pointed, and scanned the shelves for a jar of Thursday.

'Yes. We could buy it, but I prefer to use the indirect route. It's more satisfying.' Mr Smith surveyed the laboratory, beaming.

'Who works here? Is it Mr Robinson?'

'No, no.' He patted my hand. 'Mr Robinson is not concerned with this side of the business. Now, before we go any further —' He kissed me on the mouth, and it was all I could do not to push him away. 'I've been longing to ever since I saw you in that dress . . . Esmeralda.'

'What should I call you, please?' I gabbled, hoping to distract him.

'My first name is Theodore. Few people know it; I prefer to be anonymous Mr Smith. We are alike, you and I, hiding in plain sight. From the moment I met you, though, I knew you were far from ordinary; a woman passing in a man's world...'

'Is that what you will want me to do?'

'I wouldn't ask you to. Now you can be yourself.' Despite the corset and petticoats, I flinched when his hand touched my waist. He snatched it away, frowning.

'I'm sorry, I wasn't expecting —'

'No, I should have realised.' He put his hand back on my waist. 'I have sought someone like you for years. Someone who understands me, who has been overlooked as I have. Someone who will take their place by my side and share my success. That is what I want you to do.' His bright brown eyes looked deep into mine. 'Could you?'

I trembled under his gaze, fearing that my face would give me away. The blood in my veins ran like ice. But I could not escape, for I had not seen enough. And what would he do if I said no? 'Yes,' I whispered. 'Yes.'

His arms crushed me in his embrace, and my heart thumped as I tried to respond to his kiss. 'My darling Esmeralda! Now you are mine, I shall show you the best of all.'

The next door opened onto a flight of steps leading down to a baize-covered door. As we descended I heard a faint clanking. 'I apologise for the noise.' Mr Smith opened the door and behind it was another. The clanking was far louder now. He took a skeleton key from his pocket and inserted it in the lock.

I gasped. It was a factory, but there were no people. There were only machines. Bottles travelled along a moving track leading to two huge metal vats. The bottles were filled, corked, labelled and boxed, all by machine. I tried to read the labels on the bottles, but they were turned away from me. The heat was stifling; yet I felt even colder. 'It's all automatic,' shouted Mr Smith. 'No-one to steal my ideas. No-one to betray me.'

'But . . . Mr Robinson?'

'Come away.' The noise lessened as he shut the doors. He put his hands on my bare shoulders. 'There is no Mr Robinson.' A red spark danced in his smiling eyes. 'It's all me. It always was. This wonderful scheme is all mine. And by the time people realise what I've done, it will be too late.'

He leaned in to kiss me again and I pushed him away so hard that he stumbled. The smile on his face flashed into rage. I pulled the whistle from my bodice and blew with all my breath, before I turned and ran.

Chapter 18

Ingenious, Ingenious

'I don't like it at all,' said Holmes, striding so fast that I had to run to keep up.

'It's been forty minutes, and you said an hour.'

'I know what I said.'

Huggins and one of the policemen were approaching us, ready to patrol past the club. Holmes raised a hand in greeting, and we drew to one side. 'I think we should go in,' he muttered.

'I do too,' said Huggins. The policeman nodded, and all eyes turned to me.

'It's not the plan we agreed,' I said, defensively.

'Watson, walk with me.' We turned back the way we had come. 'I already feel the creeping fear that possesses me whenever I hear the name Moriarty. I worry that if we delay much longer, it will take me over.'

'But Moriarty isn't involved —'

'That's what horrifies me; the possibility of another man in the world as evil as Moriarty.'

We walked in silence till we spied Lestrade and Fingers Molloy strolling towards us. 'It's time,' Holmes muttered. 'Huggins, run for the others.'

Three minutes later we were assembled in front of a shabby blue door. Fingers stepped forward, placed his hand on the door and whistled the tune, and the door gave under his hand. 'Ingenious, ingenious,' whispered Lestrade, a savage joy on his face.

'Quiet, everyone, and guns at the ready,' whispered Holmes. We crept downstairs, expecting an ambush at any moment, and Holmes listened at the door. 'I hear nothing, but . . . on the count of three.'

We burst into an empty, palatial room. A tray of drinks stood on a table. 'This can't be it!' hissed Lestrade. 'Has she tricked us and helped him escape?'

The shriek rang through me like an electric shock. 'She's beneath us!' cried Holmes. 'Fingers, is there another way out? A secret door?'

'I don't know of one,' muttered Fingers. He had gone as white as a sheet. 'If I had thought — '

'No time for that now,' said Holmes. 'Try the walls, the floor, the mirrors —' He gasped as the whistle blared again, louder. 'She is closer!'

We ran to the walls and pulled, pushed, prodded, wrenched. Lestrade ripped a mirror from the wall. One policeman twisted at a light fitting, while another pulled up the carpet. Holmes strode alongside the wall, tapping it with his knuckles and frowning. 'Ah! Hollow!' He ran his fingers along the moulding, around the mirror… 'Not another sound lock — ha!' A panel swung round, and we surged forward.

Holmes opened the first door, and stopped dead. 'Her clothes!' He slammed the door shut and ran on, and we were hot on his heels. A workshop, a laboratory, orderly and empty. Holmes opened the final door —

A piercing scream rang out. We clattered down the steps and Holmes cried in dismay as the door gave onto another. He rattled the handle. 'Locked!' He shouldered it, but the door was solid. Beyond it was a mechanical clanking.

'Here!' Fingers pushed forward, undoing his canvas roll. He rammed the skeleton key into the lock.

I will never forget the scene that met our eyes. In front of a metal vat stood a woman in a ripped green dress, her hands behind her head. With horror, I recognised Jack. Her chest heaved, but she was silent. Her gaze slid from us towards —

'You!' I shouted.

'Ah yes. Dr Watson, isn't it? I hope you enjoyed your tonic.' The healthy glow in his cheeks had turned into an angry flush, and his pistol was aimed above Jack's head, at the vat. 'Don't even think about shooting, or your little friend will meet a death such as you cannot imagine. Put your guns on the floor, and push them away with your foot.' He watched us with his bright brown eyes. 'Better.' He paused. 'I'm surprised you're here, Fingers. Or did she play up to you, too?'

Fingers' face was a mask of fury. 'What is this?' He flung an arm at the machinery clanging away, and the bottles of red liquid I knew all too well. 'What is it all?'

'What's in that tonic?' I cried, my stomach churning.

'You're quite all right, doctor,' said Mr Smith. 'The bottle I gave you was from batch A. I take a version of it myself, except mine doesn't have the touch of opium in it. It's batch B you should be careful of. Shouldn't you, Jack?'

Jack's eyes implored us, silently. I felt Huggins step back.

'I take it batch B contains the uranium,' Holmes spat.

'A little, among other things,' said Mr Smith. 'Just enough to weaken, to decay. But in the long run…'

'My God,' I muttered. 'You want to poison the world.'

'Yes, I do! The portion of it foolish enough to trust in quack remedies, at any rate. That's part of the plan.' Mr Smith smiled. 'But I don't have time to stand gossiping with you. This vat Jack is standing by is full of superheated, undiluted batch B. Turn round, dear, and look at it.' Jack turned, her shoulders shaking. 'If I shoot the vat, she will suffer such burns… Of course you don't know what a radiation burn is. But you won't recognise her afterwards. Oh, and her lungs will burn too. She won't die at once, though. She'll live long enough to understand what a stupid, cowardly decision she made when she chose you over me.' His voice hardened. 'So I shall take you to a nice little holding room and lock you in while I make my escape; keeping Jack as my hostage, of course. If one of you puts a foot wrong — well, how Jack will wish I had shot her. Fingers, show me your skeleton key and throw it over. Then roll your toolkit towards me. You won't be needing that again.'

Fingers Molloy tugged the canvas roll from his pocket, opened it, and took out the key. He held it up, and tossed it into the air. Our eyes followed the shining arc, and —

Mr Smith staggered backwards, flailing, utter surprise on his face. A thin trickle of blood ran from his forehead. He fell against a belt of moving bottles which carried him along for a moment, then collapsed, twitching, on the floor. A few bottles crashed down with him, the red liquid spreading like blood. His movements grew weaker and weaker until finally Mr Smith, his brown eyes fixed and staring, lay still.

'I was waiting for a distraction,' said Huggins.

'But how did you —?' gasped Lestrade.

'I always carry a spare.' Huggins stowed the tiny pistol carefully in his waistband. 'And today I'm glad of it.' He went to Jack, who stood like a statue. 'Are you all right?'

Jack lowered her arms, and turned away from the vat. Her eyes moved to the body slumped on the floor, and she wrenched at her plait. 'No.' She threw it down and ripped the necklace from her throat. 'No, I'm not all right. Don't touch me!' she shrieked, as Fingers hurried towards her.

Lestrade rubbed his forehead. 'Let's turn this infernal thing off.' He prowled around the clanking, relentless beast. 'Holmes, there's a big red button marked OFF. Do you think it's safe to push it?'

'Who knows,' Holmes muttered, surveying the scene. 'Who knows.'

'Here goes nothing...' We held our breath as the machine slowed, and ground to a halt. The silence filled the room.

Holmes inspected the crimson puddle on the floor. 'We had better secure this place. This should be the harmless stuff, but better to be careful.' He collected a bottle from each conveyor belt. 'I shall leave the analysis of this to a specialist.'

'I'll wire the Yard for reinforcements.' Lestrade turned to the policemen. 'Could you stay on duty till we can get more men?' They nodded and walked over to the pile of guns.

'Jameson might come back,' Jack said. Her voice was flat. 'He was here earlier.'

'He won't put up much of a fight,' said Fingers.

'Two men behind the front door should do it,' said Lestrade.

'One here as well,' called Holmes from the other side of the room. He indicated a plain white door. 'Locked, but I imagine this is the escape route.'

'The skeleton key would open it,' said Fingers.

'It can wait for now.' Holmes sighed. 'We have seen enough evil for one day. Let us go.'

Jack took a step, wobbled, and would have fallen if Huggins had not caught her. He set her back on her feet. 'Steady, now,' he said. 'I expect you'll be glad to get those shoes off.'

'Are my clothes still upstairs?' she asked. Huggins nodded. 'Thank God for that.' She shivered, and took his arm.

No one spoke as we climbed the stairs, or as we stood in the ruined round room waiting for Jack. We emerged into the alley and Lestrade shook hands with us all. 'I'll keep you informed. Huggins, are you coming back with me?'

Huggins looked at Lestrade, then at Jack. 'I can stay if you need me,' he said, gently.

Jack's suit was still smart, but she was crumpled inside it. 'I can manage,' she snapped, pulling her arm away.

'What about these three?' Lestrade waved a hand at Fingers, Jack and Snell. 'They can't go back to Upper Wimpole Street, not without a guard.'

'We'll take them to Baker Street,' said Holmes.

'I'm not sure where we'll put them all, but I am sure Mrs Hudson can provide. Better than a prison cell, anyway.'

Fingers shivered. 'That's very kind of you, sir.'

Holmes regarded him sternly. 'No funny business though, Fingers. Don't make me count the spoons.' He walked onto Charing Cross Road and hailed a cab. 'Watson, can you deliver these three. I shall walk. I would like to be alone for a while.'

As the cab rattled away I almost failed to recognise Holmes. His head was bowed, his shoulders drooped. I would have taken him for twenty years older.

Chapter 19

Endings And Beginnings

I put the pen down and rubbed my tired eyes. Half-past five. I blotted the sheet and made all tidy, then closed and locked the office door.

As was my custom, I knocked on Inspector Lestrade's door to say goodnight. He turned the paper he was reading face-down. 'All in order, Jack?' He met my eyes, and smiled.

'Yes, sir. I'll see you tomorrow.'

***

The Inspector needn't have worried that I would look at the paper; it was more than my job was worth. It had taken me some days to recover from the events at the Gentleman's Retreat. The people at Baker Street were more than kind, but as I returned to something like my normal self I realised I had no home, no job, and little money. The thought of starting again threw me into despair, and I began to search for situations vacant with a heavy heart. The note from Inspector Lestrade inviting me to discuss Mr Huggins's former post was a blessing.

'It won't be exciting,' he had cautioned. 'You'll be alone with the files most of the time.'

'I have had more than enough excitement for now,' I said. 'There is one thing…'

'What is it?'

'What am I expected to wear?'

He snorted. 'You can wear a bathing dress or a fireman's uniform, so long as you do the work!'

After turning the question over for hours and reaching no satisfactory conclusion, I confided in Mrs Hudson. She took me to her sitting room, assured me that tight-lacing, giant bustles and high-heeled boots were not compulsory, and offered an appointment with her dressmaker. It is still far more clothing than I am used to wearing, but I am growing accustomed to it. My hair is nearly to my shoulders now, when it is down.

I saw little of Sherlock Holmes during my days at 221B Baker Street. He enquired after my health when our paths crossed, but he was busy directing operations at the Gentleman's Retreat. Dr Watson let slip that the plain white door in the basement had led to another suite of rooms, including a library filled with science and engineering works, as well as several notebooks containing schemas and plans. The corridor had ended two streets away, in a disused mews.

Several scholarly men came to visit Mr Holmes at Baker Street. One, a Professor MacTaggart, had a particularly penetrating voice. 'I can't believe it!' he boomed from the parlour below. 'Teddy Smith! When he was in my team at Oxford we humoured his crackpot schemes. Such a pleasant, jolly chap…'

Mr Holmes' voice murmured in response.

'The tonic? Ha! The first bottle was a typical quack remedy, with a limited medicinal value. The second — a regular dose would kill an invalid within a year. The man made some scientific breakthroughs; but how I wish he had not!' The Professor's voice cracked as he spoke.

Later that afternoon I was reading in the kitchen when Mr Holmes took a seat opposite me. 'I imagine you heard most of the Professor's discourse earlier.'

'I could scarcely avoid it.'

'The sad thing is that his genius — for it was genius — was not used for good. Lestrade has already commissioned a master craftsman to make tool-rolls for Scotland Yard. The rest…' He stared into the fire for some moments. 'The rest will be destroyed.'

A small black diary was recovered from the body, containing several appointments. When I began my work at Scotland Yard, one of my first tasks was to organise and file the many reports and charge sheets arising from those meetings. Inspector Lestrade and Constable Huggins picked the men off one by one, as they entered the Gentleman's Retreat, and found they had been as much in the dark about the true nature of Mr Smith's operation as Fingers Molloy.

On the first day I managed to leave my room, I met Fingers on the landing. He was wearing his overcoat, and carrying a small suitcase. 'I hate goodbyes,' he said. 'But as I dragged you into all this, it's only decent.'

'Where are you going?'

'My sister and her husband 'ave got a farm outside Eastbourne. I reckon some fresh country air will do me good, after all this.' His coat and hat were as smart as ever, but Fingers himself was a little smaller, a bit more wizened.

'Won't you miss London?'

'Yus.' Fingers rubbed his chin. 'I'll miss the London I knew before I got into all this.' He grinned. 'Anyway, I can always come up for the day and take old Snell out on the town.'

'What's he going to do?'

'He's had enough too. Mrs Hudson has recommended him for an under-butler at a place she knows, and he's bound to behave himself.' Fingers consulted his watch. 'Train to catch. Goodbye, Jack. Mr Holmes has my address, if you want to write. Might take me a while to write back, mind.' The door closed behind him with barely a click.

When I had grown a little more used to skirts, I took a room in a boarding-house an omnibus ride away from Scotland Yard. Mr Holmes promised he would come and say hello to me at the Yard, and even Dr Watson seemed a little sad at my departure. 'Take care of yourself, Jack,' he said, gruffly.

'Take care of Mr Holmes,' I replied. 'Do you think he'll be all right?'

'When he gets a new case.' Dr Watson sighed.

I settled in quickly at Scotland Yard. For the first fortnight I was given light work; filing and fair copies. I was bent over a cabinet when a quiet 'Hullo' made me jump. It was Huggins, uniformed and shiny-buttoned. 'How are you getting on?'

'It makes a nice change from my previous work.' I closed the drawer and sat at my desk. 'Are you enjoying your new job?'

He perched on the edge of the desk and considered. 'Yes . . . although it's a bit, well, quiet, at the moment. No night visits to the British Museum, no secret underground dens. Not so far, anyway.'

'Don't remind me.'

'I'm sorry, J —' He frowned. 'What should I call you? I never learnt your surname.'

'I wasn't sure what to call myself, at first. I've had so many names.'

'Really? How come?' He checked himself. 'You don't have to say, if you'd rather not...' His cheeks were a little pink. But I already knew it would be all right.

I took a deep breath. 'Until I was ten, my name

was Martha Day. I left the workhouse to be a maid, and the matron gave me the note my mother had left with me at the orphanage. That's how I learnt my real name was Jacinth. When I started as a maid I was Mary, as that was always the name of the youngest maid. And when I ran away to London, well, lots of boys are called Jack, and it was close to my real name. Hargreaves I got from a newspaper.'

'That is an awful lot of names,' said Huggins. 'But I still don't know what to call you.' He gave me a sheepish smile.

I smiled back and held out my hand. 'My name is Miss Jacinth Day.'

'And I am Constable Tom Huggins.' He took my hand and bowed. 'Pleased to make your acquaintance.'

***

'Goodnight, Miss Day,' said the policeman on duty outside. I stepped into the street and, as on most evenings, Tom Huggins was standing beneath a lamp-post nearby, his buttons gleaming in the late-afternoon sun.

'I happened to be in the area.' He offered his arm. 'May I walk you to your omnibus?'

'That would be very kind.' I took it, and we strolled down the street together. 'Would you care for a cup of coffee on the way?'

Sometimes the cup of coffee leads to a walk in the park, sometimes an early supper, sometimes even the theatre. We always have plenty to talk about; our work, Mr Holmes's latest case, the occasional letter from Fingers. We stroll in the grand streets of London, and recall the time we spent in Upper Wimpole Street, and, of course, 221B Baker Street. But the one place we never go near is the alley behind Charing Cross Road, where there is a gap like a missing tooth, and the squeezebox man plays no more.

Acknowledgements

Roll credits!

First of all, thank you to everyone who read and commented on the manuscript of *A Jar of Thursday*: Brian S Creek, Ruth Cunliffe, Judith Leask, Gaynor Seymour, Adela Torres and Georgina Walker.

As ever, John Croall provided eagle-eyed proofreading skills, and on this occasion also saved me from falling down a time-related wormhole! Any remaining errors are down to me.

I would also like to thank Nickianne Moody of Liverpool John Moores University for allowing me access to the Liddell Hart Collection of Costume, where I spent a delightful day researching late-Victorian fashion (and just about managed not to be tempted by the Femorabilia archives nearby!). You can find out more about these fascinating archives at https://eccentricarchive.wordpress.com.

Huge thanks to the late Sir Arthur Conan Doyle, the original creator.

But as usual, the biggest thanks are to my husband Stephen Lenhardt. Not just for his support and beta-reading; *A Jar of Thursday* wouldn't exist without him. The story it springs from, 'Sherlock Holmes and the Burglar', originally had a different ending which I rewrote after beta-reader feedback. His first comment on reading the new version was 'You can't leave it like that; you have to write another story about what happens at the other end!' I replied that I would, but later… It seems very strange to think that originally I planned to write just one Sherlock Holmes story, which is the one that I plan to publish next!

Finally, thank you for reading *A Jar of Thursday*. I hope you've enjoyed reading it as much as I enjoyed writing it, and if you would like to leave a short review on Amazon, Goodreads or elsewhere, I'd really appreciate it.

Font and image credits

Script font: Lovers Quarrel by TypeSETit: https://www.fontsquirrel.com/fonts/lovers-quarrel. License — SIL Open Font License v.1.10: http://scripts.sil.org/OFL

Classic font: Libre Baskerville by Impallari Type: https://www.fontsquirrel.com/fonts/libre-baskerville. License — SIL Open Font License v.1.10: http://scripts.sil.org/OFL

Jar (recoloured and stretched): Jam The Jar by Engin_Akyurt (public domain): https://pixabay.com/en/jam-the-jar-macro-color-sweet-2333414/

Cover created using GIMP image editor: www.gimp.org.

About The Author

Liz Hedgecock grew up in London, England, did an English degree, and then took forever to start writing. After several years working in the National Health Service, some short stories crept into the world. A few even won prizes. Then the stories began to grow longer…

Now Liz travels between the nineteenth and twenty-first centuries, murdering people. To be fair, she does usually clean up after herself.

Liz's Sherlock Holmes reimaginings, her Pippa Parker cozy mystery series, and the Caster & Fleet Victorian mystery series (with Paula Harmon) are available in ebook and paperback.

Liz lives in Cheshire with her husband and two sons, and when she's not writing or child-wrangling you can usually find her reading, messing about on Twitter, or cooing over stuff in museums and art galleries. That's her story, anyway, and she's sticking to it.

Website/blog: http://lizhedgecock.wordpress.com
Facebook: http://www.facebook.com/lizhedgecockwrites
Twitter: http://twitter.com/lizhedgecock
Goodreads: https://www.goodreads.com/lizhedgecock

Books by Liz Hedgecock

Short stories
The Secret Notebook of Sherlock Holmes
Bitesize

Halloween Sherlock series (novelettes)
The Case of the Snow-White Lady
Sherlock Holmes and the Deathly Fog
The Case of the Curious Cabinet

Sherlock & Jack series (novellas)
A Jar Of Thursday
Something Blue
A Phoenix Rises

Mrs Hudson & Sherlock Holmes series (novels)
A House Of Mirrors
In Sherlock's Shadow

Pippa Parker Mysteries (novels)
Murder At The Playgroup
Murder In The Choir
A Fete Worse Than Death
Murder In The Meadow

Caster & Fleet Mysteries (with Paula Harmon)
The Case of the Black Tulips
The Case of the Runaway Client
The Case of the Deceased Clerk
The Case of the Masquerade Mob
The Case of the Fateful Legacy
The Case of the Crystal Kisses

Printed in Great Britain
by Amazon